William Shakespeare's Measure for Measure: A Retelling in Prose

David Bruce

Published by David Bruce, 2022.

WILLIAM SHAKESPEARE'S MEASURE FOR MEASURE: A RETELLING IN PROSE

First edition. July 27, 2022.

ISBN: 979-8201645540

Written by David Bruce.

Table of Contents

Dedication

Dedicated to My Uncle Reuben Saturday

When he was a young man, my mother's brother Reuben wanted to escape from poverty and lard sandwiches, so he tried to run away from it. He stole a car so he could drive up north where he hoped to find opportunity, but he got caught and ended up on a Georgia chain gang for several months. In a chain gang, prisoners are shackled every few feet by the ankles to a long length of chain to keep them from escaping. They work in the hot sun while shackled to the chain, and when they sleep, they are shackled to the bed. No freedom, hard work, hot sun, no pay, bad food, and some mean guards.

When my uncle got released from the chain gang, he hitchhiked up north. He did what a lot of people trying to escape from poverty do: He drifted. He drifted from town to town, seeking opportunity and not finding it. He worked when he could, but the jobs were temporary and low pay. My uncle slept rough often, and he was hungry often. Once, when he was completely broke and completely hungry, he saw a restaurant with a buffet and went inside and asked to speak to the manager. He said, "I am very hungry, I don't have any money, and I would appreciate it very much if you would give me any food that the restaurant is going to throw away. I will be happy to wait by the rear entrance until you are ready to throw away food."

The manager told him to sit down at a table, and then the manager went to the buffet, loaded a big plate high with food, and gave it to him free of charge.

One way out of poverty is to get a good job, and my uncle got out of poverty by getting a job working with sheet metal.

My uncle's work ethic helped him. His employer sent him to California to do some special sheet-metal work, and the people in California wanted to keep him there. They explained that their California employees liked to come to work late, leave early, and take many days off. It was difficult to get someone who would show up and do the work they were supposed to do and were paid to do.

My uncle was also good with money. He got married, bought a house, and raised six children. Each time he made a mortgage payment, he paid extra money so he could pay off the mortgage faster.

If there was a sale on food, he bought lots of it. For example, if there was a sale on peanut butter, two jars for the price of one, he would buy twelve jars and sometimes go back the next day and buy six more jars.

If you went in his pantry — a closet set aside to store food — you saw that it was packed with food. If you went in his kitchen, you saw that he had taken off the doors of the high cabinets in which he stored food so that he could see the food. If you went in his bedroom, you saw that he had all the regular bedroom furniture, but he also had lots of shelves he had installed. The shelves were loaded with things that he had bought on sale that he knew his family could use: food (of course), light bulbs, toothpaste, toilet paper, etc. His bedroom looked like a warehouse.

Once he made a bad purchase: he bought a case of baked beans. Beans are beans, but the sauce they came in can taste good or bad, and the sauce these beans came in tasted bad. His kids told him, "Dad, throw those beans away! They're awful!"

But when you grow up poor, you don't throw beans away. For a long time, whenever my uncle and his family ate baked beans, they ate a mixture of one can of good baked beans and one can of bad baked beans.

My uncle's kids never had to eat lard sandwiches.
***
The doing of good deeds is important. As a free person, you can choose to live your life as a good person or as a bad person. To be a good person, do good deeds. To be a bad person, do bad deeds. If you do good deeds, you will become good. If you do bad deeds, you will become bad. To become the person you want to be, act as if you already are that kind of person. Each of us chooses what kind of person we will become. To become a good person, do the things a good person does. To become a bad person, do the things a bad person does. The opportunity to take action to become the kind of person you want to be is yours.

Educate Yourself
Read Like A Wolf Eats
Be Excellent to Each Other
Books Then, Books Now, Books Forever

***

In this retelling, as in all my retellings, I have tried to make the work of literature accessible to modern readers who may lack some of the knowledge about mythology, religion, and history that the literary work's contemporary audience had.

Do you know a language other than English? If you do, I give you permission to translate this book, copyright your translation, publish or self-publish it, and keep all the royalties for yourself. (Do give me credit, of course, for the original retelling.)

I would like to see my retellings of classic literature used in schools, so I give permission to the country of Finland (and all other countries) to give copies of this book to all students forever. I also give permission to the state of Texas (and all other states) to give copies of this book to all students forever. I also give permission to all teachers to give copies of this book to all students forever.

Teachers need not actually teach my retellings. Teachers are welcome to give students copies of my eBooks as background material. For example, if they are teaching Homer's *Iliad* and *Odyssey*, teachers are welcome to give students copies of my *Virgil's* Aeneid: *A Retelling in Prose* and tell students, "Here's another ancient epic you may want to read in your spare time."

MATTHEW 7:1-5

King James Version (KJV)

1 Judge not, that ye be not judged.

2 For with what judgment ye judge, ye shall be judged: and with what measure ye mete, it shall be measured to you again.

3 And why beholdest thou the mote that is in thy brother's eye, but considerest not the beam that is in thine own eye?

4 Or how wilt thou say to thy brother, Let me pull out the mote out of thine eye; and, behold, a beam is in thine own eye?

5 Thou hypocrite, first cast out the beam out of thine own eye; and then shalt thou see clearly to cast out the mote out of thy brother's eye.

1599 Geneva Bible (GNV)

We may not give judgment of our neighbors.

1 Judge not, that ye be not judged.

2 For with what judgment ye judge, ye shall be judged, and with what measure ye mete, it shall be measured unto you again.

3 And why seest thou the mote, that is in thy brother's eye, and perceivest not the beam that is in thine own eye?

4 Or how sayest thou to thy brother, Suffer me to cast out the mote out of thine eye, and behold, a beam is in thine own eye?

5 Hypocrite, first cast out that beam out of thine own eye, and then shalt thou see clearly to cast out the mote out of thy brother's eye.

CAST OF CHARACTERS

MALE CHARACTERS

VINCENTIO, the Duke of Vienna.

ANGELO, Lord Deputy in the Duke's absence.

ESCALUS, an old Lord, joined with Angelo in the deputation.

CLAUDIO, a young Gentleman.

LUCIO, a Fantastic. Lucio often talks when he should keep his mouth shut.

Two other Gentlemen similar to Lucio.

VARRIUS, a Gentleman attending on the Duke.

PROVOST. The job of a Provost is to apprehend, keep in custody, and punish criminals.

THOMAS and PETER, two Friars.

A Justice.

ELBOW, a simple Constable.

FROTH, a foolish Gentleman.

POMPEY BUM, Tapster to Mistress Overdone.

ABHORSON, an Executioner.

BARNARDINE, a dissolute Prisoner.

FEMALE CHARACTERS

ISABELLA, sister to Claudio.

MARIANA, betrothed to Angelo.

JULIET, beloved of Claudio.

FRANCISCA, a Nun.

MISTRESS OVERDONE, a Bawd.

MINOR CHARACTERS

Lords, Officers, Citizens, Boy, and Attendants.

SCENE

Vienna.

CHAPTER 1

— 1.1 —

In a room in the Duke of Vienna's palace, Duke Vincentio and Escalus, an important advisor, were speaking. Other lords were also present.

"Escalus," Duke Vincentio said.

"My lord."

"If I were to explain to you the essential qualities of ruling, I would appear to be in love with hearing myself talk. I know that your knowledge of that subject exceeds the boundaries of all the advice that my intellectual powers can give you. No more remains but that to your competence is added power that is as ample as your worth, and then your power and your competence can work together.

"You are as well versed in the nature of our people, the established laws and customs of our city, and the conditions for administering general justice as learning and practical experience has made anyone whom we can remember."

Duke Vincentio handed Escalus a document and said, "There is our commission for you, from which we would not have you deviate."

Duke Vincentio had highly praised Escalus' knowledge of government, and yet he was not going to let Escalus be the main ruler of Vienna during his absence. For that position, he had a different man in mind.

Duke Vincentio, using the royal plural, said to one of the other lords, "Call Angelo to come here before us."

The lord exited to carry out his task.

Duke Vincentio asked Escalus, "What do you think Angelo will be like as my representative when I am gone? You need to know that we have with special soul — after careful intellectual and spiritual consideration — selected him to be the ruler of Vienna in our absence. We have lent him our terror, dressed him with our love, and given his deputation all the organs of our own power. As my deputy, he will have all my power to give capital punishment, to show mercy, and to do all the things that we do as Duke of Vienna.

"What do you think about Angelo ruling Vienna in my absence?"

"If anyone in Vienna is worthy to undertake such ample grace and honor, it is Lord Angelo," Escalus replied.

"Angelo is coming," Duke Vincentio said.

Angelo entered the room.

"I am always obedient to your grace's will," Angelo said, "and I have come to know your pleasure. What do you want me to do?"

"Angelo, there is a kind of behavior in your life that to the observer fully unfolds your history. By looking at you and by observing your actions, people know that you are a man of good character. However, your virtuous attributes do not belong to you; they are not to be indulged in and enjoyed by only an individual. Heaven does with us as we do with torches. We do not light them only for ourselves; instead, we use them to provide light for everyone around us. If our virtues and talents do not help the people around us, it is as if we do not have them. We cannot simply concentrate on perfecting ourselves and not try to help other people.

"Our spirits are not greatly moved unless they are moved by great deeds or great causes. We are given great qualities so that we can accomplish great things in the public sphere. Nature never lends to any of us the smallest unit of her excellence unless, like a thrifty goddess, she makes sure that she has the glory of a creditor — she makes sure that she receives thanks for the loan as well as interest for the loan. Anyone to whom Nature lends virtues and talents must use them rather than waste them.

"But I am addressing my speech to a person who can well perform the role that I am giving to him. Stay consistent to your principles, Angelo. In our absence you will take our place as ruler of Vienna. You will have the loan of all my power. You will decide whether to give death or mercy when you serve as judge; mortality and mercy in Vienna live in your tongue and heart. Old Escalus, although he was the first person I considered to take my place, is your second-in-command."

Duke Vincentio handed a document to Angelo, saying, "Take your commission."

"My good lord, let there be some more test made of my metal, before so noble and so great a figure be stamped upon it," Angelo said, holding his commission.

He was punning on "metal" and "mettle." He realized that he was young, and he wanted his mettle, or character, to be better tested before he exercised so much power. Also, Viennese coins were made of metal, and the picture of the Duke was stamped upon them.

"Let there be no more evasion of the duty that I am giving to you," Duke Vincentio replied. "We have after mature and careful consideration decided to make you ruler of Vienna in our absence; therefore, accept your honors.

"We must leave Vienna so quickly and urgently that our departure must be given priority and so I leave undiscussed important matters. We shall write to you as time and our important affairs shall allow us. We will tell you how it goes with us, and we want you to keep us informed about what happens in Vienna.

"So, fare you well, Angelo and Escalus. To both of you I leave your commissions, and I hope that you perform them well."

"Give us permission, my lord," Angelo said, "to accompany you part of the way on your journey."

"My haste to leave does not allow you to accompany me during even part of my journey," Duke Vincentio said. "Nor need you, on my honor, have to worry about accompanying me. Worry instead about governing Vienna. Your freedom to act is as my own. You can enforce or qualify the laws as to your soul seems good. You can be strict or be merciful as to you seems best.

"Give me your hand."

Duke Vincentio and Angelo shook hands.

Duke Vincentio continued, "I will leave secretly and quietly. I love the people, but I do not like to appear before them in public. That can be good public relations, but I do not relish their loud applause and vehement shouts of greeting, nor do I consider a man who enjoys such things to be of sound judgment.

"Once more, fare you well."

"May the Heavens help you accomplish your purposes!" Angelo said.

"May the Heavens conduct you in your journey and bring you back in happiness!" Escalus said.

"I thank you. Fare you well," Duke Vincentio said, and then he exited.

Escalus said to Angelo, "I shall desire you, sir, to give me permission to have free and frank speech with you. I need information. I need to find out the full extent of my power while Duke Vincentio is gone. I know that I have some power, but I do not know its strength and extent."

This was wise of Escalus. To obey the rules, you need to know what the rules are. Once Escalus knew for certain the limits of his power, he could be careful not to exceed those limits.

"The same is true of me," Angelo said. "Let us withdraw together, and both of us should soon know how much power we have."

"I will go with your honor," Escalus said.

They left to consult the commissions that Duke Vincentio had given to them.

On a street in Vienna, Lucio and two gentlemen talked.

Lucio said, "If the Duke of Vienna with the other Dukes does not reach an agreement with the King of Hungary, why then all the Dukes will fight the King."

"Heaven grant us its peace, but not the King of Hungary's!" the first gentleman said.

"Amen!" the second gentleman said.

Peace is a good thing for most people, but for a soldier it can be a bad thing. No war equals no work, no work equals no pay, and no pay equals no food. Unemployed soldiers in their society were often called Hungarians because they were hungry.

Lucio said to the second gentleman, "You speak like the sanctimonious pirate who went to sea with the Ten Commandments, but he erased one commandment out of the tablet."

"Would that commandment be 'Thou shalt not steal'?" the second gentlemen asked.

"Yes, that is the one he erased."

The first gentleman said, "Why, it was a commandment that commanded the captain and all the others to not follow their occupations: They went to sea to steal. There's not a soldier of us all who, in the prayer of thanksgiving said before a meal, relishes the petition that prays for peace."

"I never heard of any soldier who dislikes it," the second gentleman said.

"I believe you," Lucio said to the second gentleman, "because I think that you have never been present when grace was said."

"You don't?" the second gentleman said. "I have heard a prayer said before a meal a dozen times at least."

"The kind of grace that you heard said was in meter," the first gentleman said. "For example: Rub-a-dub-dub; thanks for the grub. Yay, God!"

"I don't think that you have ever heard grace in any form or in any language," Lucio said to the second gentleman.

The first gentleman added, "Or in any religion."

Often eager to contradict others, Lucio said to the first gentleman, "Well, why not? Grace is grace, despite all controversy; for example, you yourself are a wicked villain, despite all grace."

Lucio had shifted the meaning of "grace" from "a prayer of thanksgiving before a meal" to "God's mercy."

The first gentleman said, "A pair of shears went between us."

This image referred to scissors cutting a piece of cloth. In other words, the first gentleman was telling Lucio that they were both cut from the same cloth — both of them were wicked villains. Or, more simply, "Same to you, buddy!"

"I grant that a pair of shears went between us," Lucio said. "I am the good velvet cloth; you are the raggedy edge of the cloth that was cut off and thrown away."

"If you are velvet, you are good velvet," the first gentleman said. "You are a three-piled, aka three-layered, piece of velvet, I promise you. I would rather be a piece of an English kersey cloth — a simple, ordinary Englishman — than to be piled, as you are piled, for a French velvet."

The first gentleman was insulting Lucio. He was punning on the word "piled," one of whose meanings in their society was to be bald. ("Pile" has as one meaning soft down, which can refer to the light fuzz on the head of a bald man.) Baldness was a side effect of the venereal disease syphilis, which was known as the French disease. A French velvet was slang for a French prostitute. In other words, the first gentleman was accusing Lucio of being infected with syphilis that he had gotten from a prostitute.

The first gentleman concluded by saying, "Do I speak feelingly now?"

By "feelingly," rhe first gentleman meant "to the purpose," but Lucio deliberately mistook it as meaning "with feeling."

"I think that you do have feeling when you speak. I think that your mouth has the sores of venereal disease and each word you speak causes you to feel pain. I will drink to your health, but I will never drink out of a glass that you have drunk from lest I contract the disease from which you suffer."

"I think I have done myself wrong, have I not?" the first gentleman said. "I should not have entered a contest of insults with Lucio. He always wins."

"You have done yourself wrong," the second gentleman said, "whether you are infected with venereal disease or not."

"Look, look," Lucio said. "Madam Mitigation comes!"

He was referring to Mistress Overdone, the proprietor of a whorehouse. She mitigated, or lessened, the sexual desire of the clients who visited her whorehouse. Her name was appropriate. To "do" a woman is to have sex with her, and whores are overdone.

Lucio said, "I have purchased as many diseases under her roof as come to —"

"To what, I ask," the second gentleman said.

"Guess."

"To three thousand dolors — or dollars — a year."

"Yes, and more," the first gentleman said.

"A French crown more," Lucio said.

A French crown was a coin, but it also meant a bald head — a sign of someone suffering from the French disease.

The first gentleman said, "You are always saying that I am diseased, but you are wrong. I am healthy. I am sound."

"I disagree that you are healthy," Lucio said. "But I agree that you are sound in the way that hollow things resound when struck. Your bones are hollow — a result of the later stages of the French disease. Impiety has made a feast of you and eaten your marrow."

Mistress Overdone walked up to the three men.

Annoyed at being bested in insults by Lucio, the first gentleman said to her, "Which of your hips has the worst sciatica?"

Sciatica was a painful disease that was thought to be the result of the French disease.

Mistress Overdone ignored the question and said, "Well, well; there's one over yonder arrested and being carried to prison who was worth five thousand of you all."

"Who's that, please?" the second gentleman asked.

"Sir, he is Claudio, Signior Claudio."

"Claudio is going to prison? I don't believe it," the first gentleman said.

"You may not believe it, but it is true," Mistress Overdone said. "I saw him arrested, I saw him carried away, and what is more, within these three days his head will be chopped off."

"Despite all my fooling," Lucio said, "I do not want that to happen to Claudio. Are you sure about this?"

"I am very sure about it," Mistress Overdone said, "and the reason for Claudio to be treated like this is that he made Juliet pregnant."

Lucio said, "Believe me, this may very well be true. Claudio promised to meet me two hours ago, and he has always been very careful to keep his promises."

"Besides, you know, this is consistent with a conversation that we had earlier on this subject," the second gentleman said.

"But, most of all, this agrees with Angelo's new proclamation," the first gentleman said.

"Let's go and learn the truth about this," Lucio said.

He and the two gentlemen departed.

Mistress Overdone complained to herself, "What with the war, what with the sweating cure for people infected with syphilis, what with the gallows, and what with poverty, I am losing my customers."

Pompey walked up to Mistress Overdone, who asked him, "What's the news?"

Pompey said, "That man yonder is being carried to prison."

Wanting to find out what Pompey knew, Mistress Overdone asked him, "Well, what has he done?"

"A woman."

"But what's his offence?"

"Groping for trouts in a peculiar river," Pompey said.

"Groping for trouts" was a kind of fishing in which people felt for, aka tickled, trout in a hiding place in a river. "Peculiar" meant "private," aka a place where no fishing was allowed. Pompey meant that the man — Claudio — had been tickling where no tickling was allowed. In other words, he had committed fornication.

"What, is there a maid with child by him?" Mistress Overdone asked.

"Maid" meant "maiden," aka virgin, so Mistress Overdone should have asked about a former maid.

Pompey replied, "No, but there's a woman with maid by him."

Pompey was using language precisely. The pregnant woman's unborn baby would be a virgin. In their society, a young male virgin was sometimes called a maid. Of course, the word "maid" also referred to female virgins.

Pompey asked, "You have not heard of the proclamation, have you?"

"What proclamation, man?"

"All whorehouses in the suburbs of Vienna must be plucked down."

"And what shall become of the whorehouses in the city?"

"They shall stand for seed," Pompey replied. "They would have gone down, too, but a wise burgher made an offer for them."

Pompey enjoyed making puns. A male appendage that can stand up can be used to plant a seed in a woman's uterus. After planting the seed, the male appendage goes down.

Burghers were middle-class men with overflowing pockets. Sometimes, burghers invested in whorehouses.

Mistress Overdone asked, "But shall all our houses of resort in the suburbs be pulled down?"

"To the ground, Mistress," Pompey said.

"Why, here's a change indeed in the commonwealth!"

The commonwealth is the state of the nation, but an additional meaning is people united by a common interest. A whore and her client are united.

Mistress Overdone wondered, "What shall become of me?"

Pompey replied, "Come; don't be afraid. Good counselors lack no clients. Although you change your place of business, you need not change your trade; I'll be your tapster still. And by tapster, I mean your pimp; I will pimp your whores for you. Courage! There will be pity taken on you — you who have worn your eyes almost out in the service, you will have allowances made for you."

Mistress Overdone saw the Provost, whose job is to apprehend, keep in custody, and punish criminals, coming toward them.

Alarmed, she said, "What's going on here, Thomas Tapster? We had better leave."

Pompey looked and said, "Here comes Signior Claudio, led by the Provost to prison. The pregnant Madam Juliet is with them."

Not wanting to meet the Provost, Mistress Overdone and Pompey left.

Claudio, who was bound and obviously a prisoner, complained to the Provost, "Fellow, why are you showing me thus to the world? Take me to prison, where I am committed."

The Provost said, "I am not showing you off to the world out of meanness. Lord Angelo has ordered me to do this. It is a part of your punishment."

"Thus can the demigod Authority make us pay for our offence in full in accordance with the words of Heaven in the Bible," Claudio said. "On whom punishment falls, it falls; on whom punishment does not fall, it does not fall. Either way, justice is triumphant."

Claudio may have been thinking about Proverbs 21:15: "It is joy to the just to do judgment; but destruction *shall be* to the workers of iniquity." But Zachariah 7:9 also mentions mercy and compassion: "Thus speaketh the Lord of hosts, saying, Execute true judgment, and show mercy and compassion, every man to his brother [...]."

Lucio and the two gentlemen walked over to Claudio, the Provost, and Juliet.

"How are you, Claudio!" Lucio asked. "What is the reason for these restraints? Why are you bound?"

"The reason for these restraints is too much liberty, my Lucio," Claudio said. "Too much liberty is a surfeit, an excess. Surfeiting — eating too much — is the father of much fasting. We eat too much, and then we do not eat at all. Similarly, every immoderate use of liberty leads to restraint. Our natures pursue, like rats that gulp down ratsbane, the poison specially intended to kill them — an evil that causes them to thirst. When we drink, we die."

Claudio was correct. Many laws of Vienna had not been enforced for a long time, and so people such as Claudio had taken advantage of that. Now Vienna was entering a time in which those laws were strictly enforced.

"If I could speak so wisely while I was under arrest, I would send for certain of my creditors so that they could have me arrested," Lucio said, "and yet, joking aside, I would rather have the foolishness of freedom than the wisdom of imprisonment. What offence have you committed, Claudio?"

"I have committed an offense that, if I were to mention it, would cause offense again."

"What, is it murder?" Lucio asked.

"No."

"Lechery?"

"You can call it that," Claudio said.

The Provost said to Lucio, "Leave us, sir!"

He then said to Claudio, "You must go now."

Claudio said to the Provost, "Let me speak one word, good friend."

He then said, "Lucio, a word with you."

"A hundred, if they'll do you any good," Lucio said. "Is lechery such a concern? Is lechery something that officers of the law really concern themselves with?"

"In my case, they have," Claudio said. "I had a true contract to legally marry Juliet. Because of that true contract, I got possession of Juliet's bed. You know the lady; she is definitely my wife, except that we have not had the wedding ceremony. We put off the wedding ceremony because we were hoping to get a bigger dowry out of the coffer of her family. We thought it best to hide our love for each other until we had time to get them to approve of our love for each other. But it so happens that our most mutual entertainment in bed that we had thought to keep hidden is now written large in the belly of Juliet — that is writing that anyone can read."

"She is with child, perhaps?" Lucio said. "She is pregnant?"

"Unhappily, she is," Claudio said. "And the Duke has a new deputy to rule in his absence. This deputy rules harshly, perhaps because he is young and unused to rule or perhaps because he is treating the body public like a horse he is riding for the first time — to show the horse that he is its master, he digs his spurs in its side. I don't know whether his tyranny is due to the position that he fills or it is due to his own character. Either way, he is strictly enforcing laws that have been ignored for nineteen years. These neglected laws were like unpolished armor that was hung on the wall and never worn. But now, the new deputy is strictly enforcing these half-asleep and neglected laws. He is surely doing this to earn a reputation."

"I am sure that you are right," Lucio said. "The penalty for fornication is death by beheading. Your head stands so insecurely on your shoulders that a milkmaid, if she is in love, may sigh with lovesickness and blow it off. Send after Duke Vincentio and appeal to him for mercy."

"I have tried to do that, but Duke Vincentio is nowhere to be found," Claudio said. "Please, Lucio, do me this kind service. Today my sister is supposed to enter a cloister and become a novice. Tell her the danger that I am in. Implore her, for me, to become friends with the strict deputy. Tell her to talk to him in person and try to persuade him to be lenient toward me. I have great hope in that because in her youth she has an eager and speechless dialect, a certain body language, that moves men. Besides, she uses reason and conversation well; she is very persuasive."

"I hope that she is," Lucio said, "not just for you, but for other people who have done what you have done and who would be arrested and punished just like you. You should be enjoying your life. I would hate for you to lose your life because of a game of tick-tack."

Tick-tack was a board game in which pegs were inserted into holes. The symbolism is obvious.

"I will go and see and talk to your sister," Lucio said.

"I thank you, good friend Lucio," Claudio said.

"I will see her within two hours."

Claudio said to the Provost, "Come, officer, let's leave!"

In a room in a Viennese monastery, Duke Vincentio and Friar Thomas talked.

"No, holy father; throw away that thought. Don't believe that the dribbling dart of love — a weakly shot arrow from Cupid — can pierce a bosom completely protected by armor," Duke Vincentio said.

Friar Thomas had been afraid that Duke Vincentio had come to the monastery to arrange to consummate a love affair there.

Duke Vincentio continued, "Why I want you to allow me to hide myself in a friar's habit has a purpose more grave and wrinkled and serious than the aims and ends of sexually burning youth."

"May your grace tell me that purpose?" Friar Thomas asked.

"My holy sir, none better knows than you how I have ever loved the life withdrawn from the world. I have always lightly valued haunting social gatherings where young people show off their witless and expensive clothing.

"I have given to Lord Angelo, who is a man of strict self-discipline and firm abstinence, my absolute power and position here in Vienna; he will rule Vienna until I take over again. Lord Angelo believes that I have travelled to Poland; that is a rumor that I have caused to be spread to the public, and that rumor is believed.

"Now, pious sir, do you want me to tell you why I have done this?"

"Gladly, my lord," Friar Thomas said.

"In Vienna, we have strict statutes and very biting laws. These statutes and laws are the needed bits and curbs to headstrong weeds, aka people who do not contribute to society. For fourteen years we have not enforced these statutes and laws. They are like an old lion in a cave that has convinced other lions to bring food to it. These statutes and laws and the old lion no longer bite their legitimate prey.

"Now, like foolish fathers who bound together twigs of birch to make a whip, but who merely threaten their misbehaving children with it instead of actually whipping them, with the result that the misbehaving children laugh at rather than fear the whip, so our decrees might as well not exist because they are never employed. Now, liberty grabs justice by the nose, the baby beats the nanny, and good behavior is rejected in favor of bad behavior."

"Your grace, you have always had the power to begin enforcing the laws whenever you pleased," Friar Thomas said. "Your enforcement of the laws would be more feared than Lord Angelo's enforcement because you are the Duke, not the Duke's subordinate."

"I fear that I would be too feared," Duke Vincentio said. "It is my fault that the people ceased to fear the never-enforced laws. I gave the people the freedom to ignore the laws, and I would be tyrannous if I were to suddenly and strictly enforce the laws. When we do not enforce the laws and administer punishment for breaking them, we tacitly give our approval to the general public to break those laws.

"Therefore, indeed, my father, I have on Angelo imposed the duty of enforcing the laws. Angelo may use the authority that I have lent to him to strike to the heart of the matter and enforce the laws, all without reducing my popularity with the citizens of Vienna.

"I wish to witness what Angelo does, and to do that I need a disguise. If I am disguised as a brother of your order, I can visit both Angelo and the people of Vienna; therefore, I ask you to give me the habit of a friar and to instruct me in how I may bear myself so that I act like a friar.

"More reasons for this action I will give to you when I have more time, but I will tell you now one more reason. Lord Angelo is straitlaced and puritanical, he keeps up his guard against the doing of evil, and he scarcely confesses that his blood flows or that his appetite leans more to bread than stone. He is so puritanical that it is as if he will not admit that he has human impulses. I want to see what happens to him as a result of his having my power. Will power change him? Is Angelo really what he now seems to be?"

— 1.4 —

Isabella, Claudio's sister, spoke to the nun Francisca in a nunnery of Saint Clare, the religious order that Isabella wished to join.

"Do you nuns have any farther privileges?" Isabella asked.

"Aren't these privileges enough?" Francisca replied.

"Yes, they are," Isabella said. "I don't wish for more privileges; instead, I wish for fewer privileges. I wish that the sisterhood, the votarists of Saint Clare, were under stricter restraints."

Lucio called from outside the nunnery, "Hello! May peace be in this place!"

Isabella asked, "Who's that person who is calling?"

"It is a man's voice," Francisca said. "Gentle Isabella, turn the key and open the door, and find out from him what he wants. You may talk to him; I may not. You are not yet a member of our religious order.

"When you have taken the vows, you must not speak with men except in the presence of the prioress. If you speak, you must not show your face. Or, if you show your face, you must not speak."

Lucio shouted again.

Francisca said, "He calls again; please, talk to him."

Francisca moved a short distance away.

Isabella opened the door and said, "Peace and prosperity to you! Who is it who is calling?"

Lucio entered the room and said, "Hail, virgin, if you are a virgin, as those cheek-roses of yours proclaim that you are no less! Can you help me by allowing me to see Isabella, who is a novice of this place and the fair sister of her unhappy brother Claudio?"

"Why is Claudio 'her *unhappy* brother'?" Isabella replied. "Let me ask, and let me let you know that I am Isabella, Claudio's sister."

"Gentle and fair Isabella, your brother kindly greets you," Lucio said. "To come straight to the point, he's in prison."

"That is bad news!" Isabella said. "Why is he in prison?"

"For something that, if I were his judge, his punishment ought to be thanks rather than something bad. He has gotten his lover pregnant."

"Sir, don't joke about such things," Isabella said.

"It is true," Lucio replied. "Although it is my familiar sin when I speak with maidens to make jokes and to act like the deceiving lapwing, a bird that deceives people and animals in order to lead them away from its nestlings, and to make my tongue say things that are not in my heart, I would not do such things to all virgins. You are a novice in a nunnery. I regard you as a virgin who is Heavenly and saintly. By renouncing the world, you have acquired a spirit that will be immortal in Heaven. Because of who you are, I must talk to you with complete sincerity, as if I were talking to a saint."

"When you mock me by giving me good characteristics I do not deserve, you are blaspheming the truly good," Isabella said.

"Do not believe it," Lucio said. "You deserve the respect that I am giving to you.

"In few and truthful words, this is what has happened. Your brother and his lover have embraced. Just like those who eat grow full, just like blossoming time turns seeds in fallow ground to a bountiful harvest, even so her plenteous womb expresses your brother's full tilling and husbandry. Your brother has planted his seed in her, and that seed is growing."

"My brother has gotten someone pregnant? Is she my cousin Juliet?"

"Is she really your cousin?"

"Not literally," Isabella said. "We are close friends — so close that we might as well be biologically related. We are like schoolgirls who call each other affectionate names — such things are silly but appropriate for schoolgirls."

"She is the woman whom your brother made pregnant."

"Then he should marry her."

"This is the point," Lucio said. "Duke Vincentio has very strangely gone from Vienna. He led many gentlemen, myself being one of them, to expect that there would soon be military action, but we have learned from those in the know that Duke Vincentio's public utterances were an infinite distance away from what he really means to do.

"In his place, and with all of his power and authority, he allows Lord Angelo to govern Vienna. Lord Angelo is a man whose blood is composed only of snow-broth: melted snow. Lord Angelo is a man who never feels the wanton stings and urges of sexual desire. He reduces and blunts his natural keenness of sexual desire with two things that improve the mind: studying and fasting.

"Lord Angelo wants people to fear to use the liberty that we have had recently — liberty that has ignored the hideous law, much the way that a mouse ignores a nearby lion. To do that, he has picked out a law and decided to strictly enforce it. Your brother broke that law, the punishment for which is forfeiture of his life. Lord Angelo had your brother arrested for breaking that law, and now Lord Angelo will punish your brother; that way, your brother will serve as an example to others.

"All hope is gone, unless you have the grace by your fair appeal to soften Angelo and have him reduce the punishment. That is the essence of the errand that I have run between your brother and you."

"Is Angelo really seeking to end my brother's life?"

"He has already condemned your brother, and I have heard that the Provost has the order to execute your brother."

"This is dreadful," Isabella said. "Whatever abilities and talents I have are poor and unlikely to do my brother any good."

"Gather together all the resources that are in you," Lucio said.

"My resources? I doubt —"

"Our doubts are traitors, and they make us lose the good we often might win by making us afraid to make any attempt to do what good we can," Lucio said. "Go to Lord Angelo, and let him learn that when maidens plead, men act like gods who have the power to grant them what they want — and let him learn that when maidens also weep and kneel as they plead, men give the maidens whatever they want and exactly the way the maidens want it. Maidens can be much more persuasive than you think when it comes to men."

"I'll see what I can do."

"Good, but do it quickly."

"I will get started right away," Isabella said. "I will stay here no longer than it takes to give the Mother Superior notice of this affair. I humbly thank you. Commend me to my brother. Early this evening, I will send him news about the outcome of my pleading."

"Farewell," Lucio said. "I take my leave of you."

"Good sir, *adieu*."

CHAPTER 2

— 2.1 —

Angelo, Escalus, a Justice, the Provost, and some officers and attendants were meeting in a courtroom.

Angelo said, "We must not make a scarecrow of the law, setting it up to make the birds of prey afraid but letting it remain motionless so that the birds of prey grow accustomed to it and make it their perch and not their terror."

Escalus replied, "Yes, but always let us be keen and sharp, and cut a little and prune where needed rather than let the axe fall and chop down and kill the tree. This gentleman whose life I would save — Claudio — had a most noble father!

"Your honor, whom I believe is very strict in preserving his virtue, you should realize that you yourself have sexual urges, and if the right time and right place had come along, or if the right place had come along when your sexual desire was at its height, or if you had the opportunity to act on your sexual desires and achieve the satisfaction you desired, then perhaps sometime in your life you yourself would have erred in the same way as this man whom you have sentenced to death. You yourself might have been punished in the same way by the same law."

"It is one thing to be tempted, Escalus, and another thing to fall," Angelo said. "I do not deny that the jury, passing sentence on the prisoner's life, may among the sworn twelve jurors have a thief or two who are guiltier than the prisoner on trial.

"When a crime is revealed to justice, that is the crime that justice seizes. The people who are put on trial are the people who are arrested. Who knows how many thieves have served on juries that have tried other thieves?

"It is very obvious that when we see a jewel on the ground we stoop and pick it up. We do that because we see it, but we tread upon the jewel we do not see and never think about it.

"You may not extenuate Claudio's offence because I myself have had similar sexual urges. Instead, you should tell me that if I, who have condemned Claudio, should also commit the same offense, then the judgment of death that I gave to Claudio should also be given to me with no mercy shown or extenuating circumstances being urged.

"Sir, Claudio must die."

"Be it as your wisdom will have it," Escalus replied.

"Where is the Provost?" Angelo asked.

"Here I am, if it pleases your honor," the Provost replied.

"See that Claudio is executed by nine tomorrow morning. Bring to him his confessor; let him confess his sins and be prepared to die because tomorrow morning will be the end of his Earthly pilgrimage."

The Provost departed.

Escalus thought, *May Heaven forgive Claudio — and forgive us all! Some rise because they sin, and some fall because they are virtuous. Some people walk many times on the ice of a frozen pond and crack it without falling through; other people fall through the first time they stand on ice. Similarly, some people commit many crimes without ever being caught; other people are caught the first time they commit a crime.*

Elbow, who was a Constable, and some other law officials arrived. With them were two men named Froth and Pompey, whom they had arrested. Elbow was not good with language; he committed many malapropisms in his speech.

"Come, bring them away," Elbow said. "If these two men are good people in a commonwealth who do nothing but use their abuses — do wicked things — in common whorehouses, I know no law. Bring them away."

"Greetings, sir!" Angelo said. "What's your name and what's the matter?"

"If it please your honor, I am the poor Duke's Constable, and my name is Elbow."

Elbow should have said that he was the Duke's poor Constable.

Elbow added, "I do lean upon justice, sir, and do bring in here before your good honor two notorious benefactors."

"Benefactors?" Angelo said. "Well, what benefactors are they? Aren't they malefactors?"

Angelo used words better than Elbow. Angelo knew the difference between a benefactor and a malefactor.

"If it pleases your honor, I don't know well what they are, but I do know that they are puritanical villains, that I am sure of, and I am sure that they are void of all profanation in the world that good Christians ought to have."

Most villains are not puritanical, and most good Christians are likely to think that they prefer profession — witnessing to the world about the glory of God — to profanation. However, some villains can very well be puritanical — they are hypocritical villains.

Escalus said sarcastically, "This is well said; here is a wise officer."

"Continue," Angelo said. "What is the occupation or social class of these two men?"

Elbow was slow to speak.

Angelo asked, "Elbow is your name? Why don't you speak, Elbow?"

Pompey joked, "He cannot, sir; he's out at 'Elbow.'"

Being out at elbow can mean wearing ragged clothing — clothing with holes in the elbows. Pompey also was joking that Elbow's brain went out when he heard his name — Elbow was at a loss for words when he heard his name. Chances are, Elbow simply had been distracted by something and did not hear Angelo.

"Who are you, sir?" Angelo asked Pompey. "What is your occupation or social class?"

Elbow answered for Pompey, "He, sir! He is a tapster, aka bartender, sir. He is a part-time pimp. He is a man who serves a bad woman. The bad woman's whorehouse, sir, was, as they say, plucked down in the suburbs; and now she professes to run a hot-house, which she calls a bath-house, but I think that the hot-house is a very ill house, too."

"Why do you think that?" Escalus asked.

"My wife, sir, whom I detest before Heaven and your honor —"

"Detest?" Escalus asked. "You detest your wife?"

Elbow should have said that he professes his wife — he declares that his wife is his wife.

"Yes, sir," Elbow replied. "My wife is a woman whom, I thank Heaven, is an honest and faithful woman —"

"Why then do you detest her?" Escalus asked.

Escalus knew that Elbow was making malapropisms, but Escalus was not above encouraging Elbow to make a fool of himself.

"I say, sir," Elbow replied, "I will detest myself also, as well as she, that this house, if it is not a bawd's house, it is pity of her life because it is a wicked house."

Elbow had stated that if the house under discussion is not a whorehouse, then it would be a pity for his wife.

"How do you know that the house is a whorehouse, Constable?" Escalus asked.

"Sir, I know it from my wife," Elbow replied. "If my wife had been a woman cardinally given, she might have been accused of fornication, adultery, and all moral uncleanliness there."

Instead of "cardinally," Elbow should have said, "carnally."

Elbow was complaining that Pompey had tried to recruit Mrs. Elbow as a prostitute, or perhaps he was complaining that Froth had mistaken her for a prostitute, or both.

"This would have happened because of the woman's agent — a pimp working for her?" Escalus asked.

"Yes, sir, by Mistress Overdone's agent, but as my wife spit in his face, she defied him."

Pompey said, "Sir, if it please your honor, this is not the truth."

"Prove it before these varlets here, you honorable man," Elbow said. "Prove it."

Escalus said to Angelo, "Do you hear how he misuses words? He is calling us varlets, and he is calling this alleged pimp an honorable man."

Pompey said, "Sir, his pregnant wife went into our house because she was longing, saving your honor's reverence, for stewed prunes. Sir, we had only two stewed prunes in the house, which at that very distant time stood, as it were, in a fruit dish, a dish that cost some three pence. Your honors have seen such dishes; they are not China dishes, but they are very good dishes —"

Despite being under arrest, Pompey was having fun. He was deliberately putting much irrelevant detail into his speech, and he was parodying Elbow's malapropisms by saying "distant time" instead of "exact time" or "at that instant."

"Stop wasting our time," Escalus said. "The dish does not matter, sir."

"No, indeed, sir. It does not matter a pin. You are therein in the right, but let me get to the point," Pompey said. "As I say, this Mistress Elbow, being, as I say, pregnant with child, and being great-bellied, and longing, as I said, for prunes; and us having but two in the dish, as I said, Master Froth here, this very man, having eaten the rest, as I said, and, as I say, paying for them very honestly; for, as you know, Master Froth, I could not give you three pence again."

"No, indeed," Froth replied.

"Very well," Pompey said to Froth. "You being then, if you remember, cracking the stones of the foresaid prunes —"

"Yes, so I did indeed," Froth said.

"Why, very well," Pompey said. "I told you then, if you remember, that such a one and such a one were past cure of the thing you know of, unless they kept very good diet, as I told you —"

Someone listening to Pompey could think that he was talking about prostitutes who suffered from venereal disease and who ate stewed prunes as a treatment for the disease. In fact, that is what he was talking about. Basically, he was babbling in the hope of confusing the judges so that they would decide not to punish him and Froth.

"All this is true," Froth said.

Pompey said, "Why, very well, then —"

"Come, you are a tedious fool," Escalus said. "Speak words that are to the purpose. What was done to Elbow's wife that he has cause to complain of? Come and tell me what was done to her."

"Sir, your honor cannot come to that yet," Pompey said. "'Cum' and 'done to her' — get it?"

"I am using those words with different meanings from the ones you suggest," Escalus said.

"Sir, but you shall come to it, by your honor's leave. And, I ask you, look at Master Froth here, sir. He is a man whose income is four-score pounds a year, and his father died at Hallowmas: November 1, aka All Saints' Day. It was at Hallowmas, wasn't it, Master Froth?"

"No, it was on All-Hallond Eve, aka All-Hallows Eve: October 31, aka Halloween or the Eve of All-Saints' Day."

"Why, very well," Pompey said. "I hope here we speak truths. He, sir, sitting, as I say, in a lower chair, sir; it was in the Bunch of Grapes room at the tavern, where indeed you delight to sit, don't you?"

"I do indeed," Froth said, "because it is a public room and good for winter because a fire is kept burning in it."

"Why, very well, then," Pompey said. "I hope here we speak truths."

"This will outlast a night in Russia, when nights are longest there," Angelo said to Escalus. "I'll leave now, and I will leave the hearing of the case to you, hoping that it will be the case that you'll find good reason to whip them all."

Whipping was a common legal punishment.

"I think that I will find reason to whip both men," Escalus said. "Good day to your lordship."

Angelo exited.

Escalus said to Pompey, "Now, sir, come on. Tell me what was done to Elbow's wife once more."

"Once, sir? There was nothing done to her once."

Elbow requested, "Please, sir, ask him what this man — Froth — did to my wife."

"Please, your honor," Pompey requested, "ask me."

"Well, sir; what did this gentleman do to her?"

"Please, sir, look at this gentleman's face," Pompey said.

He added, "Good Master Froth, look upon his honor; it is for a good purpose."

Pompey asked Escalus, "Does your honor see his face?"

"Yes, sir, very well."

"Please, look at his face very carefully," Pompey said.

"I am."

"Does your honor see any harm in his face?"

"Why, no."

"I'll be supposed upon a book, his face is the worst thing about him," Pompey said.

Pompey continued to parody Elbow's malapropisms. The proper expression was to be deposed, aka sworn, upon a book — the Bible. If Pompey could entertain Escalus and make Escalus like him, he might be able to escape being punished.

Pompey continued, "Good, then; if his face is the worst thing about him, how could Master Froth do the Constable's wife any harm? I would like your honor to tell me that."

"He's in the right," Escalus, who was entertained by Pompey, said. "Constable, what do you say about this?"

"First, if you don't mind," Elbow said, "the house is a respected house; next, this is a respected fellow; and his mistress is a respected woman."

Pompey knew that Elbow meant "suspected," not "respected," and he decided to have fun at Elbow's expense.

Pompey said to Escalus, "I swear by my hand, sir, his wife is a more respected person than any of us all."

"Varlet, you lie," Elbow said, rejecting the allegation that his wife was respected. "You lie, wicked varlet! The time has yet to come that my wife was ever respected by man, woman, or child."

"Sir, she was respected by him before he married her," Pompey said.

Anyone who did not know what the word "respected" meant could think that Pompey was accusing Elbow of the same crime that Claudio had been convicted of.

"Which is the wiser here?" Escalus asked, smiling. "Justice or Iniquity?"

He then asked Elbow, "Is this true?"

Elbow said to Pompey, "Oh, you caitiff! Oh, you varlet! Oh, you wicked Hannibal! I respected with her before I was married to her!"

He said to Escalus, "If ever I was respected with my wife, or she with me, let not your worship think me the poor Duke's officer."

He said to Pompey, "Prove this, you wicked Hannibal, or I'll make a charge of battery against you."

Hannibal was a Carthaginian general who brought elephants and an army across the Alps so that he could attack Rome.

Escalus, who knew the correct definitions of the words "battery" and "slander," said, "If he hits your ear, you could make a charge of slander against him, too."

"I thank your good worship for that suggestion," Elbow said. "What does your worship want me to do with this wicked caitiff?"

"Truly, officer," Escalus replied, "this man has some offences in him that you would like to discover if you could; therefore, let him continue in his courses of actions until you know what offenses he has in him."

Elbow replied, "I thank your worship."

He then said to Pompey, "You see, you wicked varlet, now, what's come upon you. You are to continue now, you varlet; you are to continue."

Escalus asked Froth, "Where were you born, friend?"

"Here in Vienna, sir."

"And do you have an income of fourscore pounds a year?"

"Yes, if it please you, sir."

"I see."

Escalus then asked Pompey, who now gave straight — or mostly straight — answers because he knew that he would not be punished, "What trade do you follow, sir?"

"I am a tapster, a poor widow's tapster."

"What is the name of the widow you work for?"

"Mistress Overdone."

"Has she had any more than one husband?"

"She has had nine husbands, sir," Pompey replied. "Overdone by the last."

"Nine!" Escalus said.

Both Pompey and Escalus smiled. "Overdone by the last" meant that she had acquired the name "Overdone" by marrying her ninth husband. However, the phrase had another meaning: Because of the nine husbands, she had been "overdone" — she was sexually exhausted.

Escalus said, "Come over here close to me, Master Froth. Master Froth, I would not have you acquainted with tapsters: They will draw you, Master Froth, and you will hang them."

The tapsters really would draw Master Froth; they would draw alcoholic beverages for him, and they would draw money away from him. As for hanging, if Master Froth continued to frequent shady bars and whorehouses, a time would come when he would be cheated and he would shout at a person such as Pompey, "Go hang yourself!"

Escalus said to Froth, "Get you gone, and let me hear no more of you."

Froth, who was happy to be let go with a warning, replied, "I thank your worship. For my own part, I never come into any room in a tap-house, but I am drawn in."

One meaning of "drawn in" is "cheated." When a tapster draws, aka pours, beer, quite frequently there is froth at the top. One way of cheating customers is to serve more froth than beer.

"Well, stay out of trouble, Master Froth," Escalus replied, "Farewell."

Froth exited.

Escalus then said to Pompey, "Come here close to me, Master Tapster. What's your name, Master Tapster?"

"Pompey."

"What is the rest of your name?"

"Bum, sir."

"Indeed, your bum is the greatest thing about you; therefore, in the beastliest sense you are Pompey the Great. Pompey, you are a part-time pimp, Pompey, although you disguise that occupation by also being a tapster, don't you? Come, tell me the truth; it shall go better for you."

"Truly, sir, I am a poor fellow who has to make a living."

"How would you make a living, Pompey? By being a pimp — a bawd? What do you think of the trade, Pompey? Is it a lawful trade?"

"It would be if the law allowed it, sir."

"But the law will not allow it, Pompey," Escalus said. "It will not be allowed in Vienna."

"Does your worship mean to geld and spay all the youth of the city? Will all the youth of the city have their testicles and ovaries removed?"

"No, Pompey."

"Truly, sir, in my poor opinion, they will go to it then. They will have sex," Pompey said.

He added, "If your worship will have the police arrest all the prostitutes and all their clients, you need not fear the pimps — they will automatically be out of their jobs."

"Some pretty serious enforcement of the laws is beginning, I can tell you. Soon there will be nothing but beheadings and hangings."

"If you behead and hang all who offend that way — who buy or sell illicit sex — for only ten years altogether, you'll be glad to give out a commission for the acquisition of more heads. If this law is enforced in Vienna for ten years, I'll rent the best house in it at a ridiculously low price — the price that I would pay today for a room the size of a closet. Rent will be very cheap because of lack of tenants. If you live to see this come to pass, say that Pompey told you so."

"Thank you, good Pompey," Escalus replied, "and, in answer to your prophecy, listen carefully to me. I advise you to not let me find you before me again in court upon any complaint whatsoever. Certainly do not let me find you before me again in court for an offense related to the place you live in today. If I see you again in this court, Pompey, I shall beat you to your tent, and I will prove to be a severe Caesar to you. Julius Caesar defeated Pompey the Great, who retreated to his tent, and I shall defeat you in court the way that Julius Caesar defeated Pompey the Great in battle. To speak plainly, Pompey, I shall have you whipped. Take this warning to heart, Pompey, and, for this time, Pompey, fare you well."

"I thank your worship for your good advice," Pompey said.

But he thought, *I shall do what flesh and fortune shall determine — they are my better advisors. Whip me? No, no; let a cartman whip his nag, or a law enforcement officer whip a whore. The valiant heart is not whipped out of his trade. I shall continue to be a part-time pimp.*

Pompey exited.

"Come over here close to me, Master Elbow," Escalus said. "Come here, Master Constable. How long have you held the job of Constable?"

"Seven years and a half, sir."

"I thought, by your readiness in the office, you had worked in it some time. You say, seven years altogether?"

"And a half, sir."

"It has been a great challenge to you," Escalus said. "They do you wrong to make you Constable so often. Aren't there men in your ward who are competent to serve as Constable?"

"Truly, sir," Elbow replied, "only a few have the intelligence to be Constable. Whenever they are chosen, they are glad to allow me to take the position. They give me some money, and I serve as Constable instead of them."

"Bring the names of some six or seven men who are the most competent in your parish."

"Should I bring the list of names to your worship's house, sir?"

"Yes, to my house," Escalus replied. "Fare you well."

Elbow exited.

Escalus asked the Justice, "What time do you think it is?"

"Eleven a.m., sir."

"Please come home and have lunch with me."

"I humbly thank you."

"I am grieved that Claudio must die, but there's no remedy for it."

"Lord Angelo is severe."

"His severity is necessary," Escalus said. "Mercy is not always mercy. Pardon is always the nurse of second woe. Being too lax in enforcing the law results in much lawlessness. But yet — poor Claudio! There is no remedy for it. Come, let us go, sir."

In a room in the courthouse, the Provost asked a servant where Angelo was.

The servant replied, "He's hearing a case; he will come here immediately after I tell him that you are here."

"Good. Please tell him I am here."

The servant departed to carry out his errand.

The Provost said to himself, "I will find out what Angelo wants to do; maybe he will relent and not sentence Claudio to death. Claudio has offended only as if he were in a dream! This is no true offense — and certainly not one that ought to be punished by death. All social classes and all ages have been guilty of committing this vice! Why should Claudio die because he committed it!"

Angelo entered the room and asked, "What's the matter, Provost?"

"Is it your will that Claudio shall die tomorrow?"

"Didn't I tell you that it is?" Angelo replied. "Haven't you received the order for Claudio's execution? Why are you asking me about Claudio's execution again?"

"I am asking in case I obey the order too quickly," the Provost said. "With your permission, let me tell you that I have seen the time when, after an execution, the judge has regretted pronouncing the death sentence."

"Ha!" Angelo said scornfully. "Let me worry about that. Do your job, or quit. If you quit, we can easily find someone to take your place."

"I beg your honor's pardon," the Provost said, adding, "What shall be done, sir, with the mourning and groaning Juliet, whom Claudio got pregnant. She is very close to her hour of giving birth."

"Take her to some place fitter for giving birth," Angelo said, "and do it quickly."

The servant returned and said, "The sister of the man who is condemned to die tomorrow is here and wishes to speak to you."

"Does Claudio have a sister?" Angelo asked.

The Provost answered, "Yes, my good lord; she is a very virtuous maiden. Soon she shall join a sisterhood and be a nun, if she has not done so already."

Angelo said, "Well, bring her here."

The servant left the room.

Angelo said to the Provost, "See that the fornicatress Juliet is moved. Let her have the necessities she requires, but don't give her anything lavish. You shall receive an order authorizing you to do this."

Isabella and Lucio entered the room.

"May God save your honor!" the Provost said.

He started to leave the room, but Angelo told him, "Stay here a little while."

To Isabella he said, "You are welcome here. What do you want?"

"I am a woeful suitor to your honor," Isabella said. "Please, your honor, listen to me. I want to ask you to do something."

"Well, what is your suit to me?"

"There is a vice that I do most abhor," Isabella said. "I most desire that this vice should meet the blow of justice. I would prefer to not plead for leniency for a person who has committed this vice, but I must do so. What I prefer to do and prefer not to do are at war."

"What are you speaking about?" Angelo asked.

"I have a brother who is condemned to die," Isabella said. "I beg you, let my brother's vice be condemned, and not my brother."

The Provost thought, *Please, Heaven, give Isabella the ability to persuade Angelo to be lenient.*

"Condemn the vice and not the person who committed the vice?" Angelo replied. "Why, every vice is condemned even before it is committed. I would only be pretending to do my duty if I were to condemn the vices and record them when they are committed and yet let the person who committed the vice go free."

"Oh, the law is just but severe!" Isabella said. "I had a brother, then. I have no brother now because he is condemned to die. May Heaven keep and preserve your honor!"

Lucio whispered to Isabella, "Don't give up so easily. Plead with him some more. Beg him. Kneel down before him, and grab and hang upon his judicial robe. You are too cold; if you should need a pin, you could not with a tamer tongue ask for it. Put some emotion in your voice! Plead with him, I say!"

"Does he have to die?" Isabella asked.

"Yes, maiden," Angelo said. "Nothing else can happen."

"I think that something else can happen," Isabella said. "I think that you might pardon him. If you were to pardon him, neither Heaven nor humans would grieve because of your mercy."

"I will not pardon him."

"Could you, if you wanted to?"

"Whatever I will not do, that I cannot do."

"But it is possible for you to do it, and if you did it, you would do the world no wrong," Isabella said. "Wouldn't you pardon him if your heart were touched with the compassion for him that I feel?"

"He has been sentenced; it is too late," Angelo replied.

Lucio whispered to Isabella, "You are too cold. You aren't showing enough emotion."

"Too late?" Isabella said. "Why, no, it is not too late. I, after I speak a word, may call it back again. I can change my mind.

"Believe this: No insignia that pertains to great ones — not the King's crown, nor the sword of justice that is given to mayors and governors, nor the marshal's truncheon, nor the judge's robe — become them with one half as good a grace as mercy does.

"Remember this proverb: It is in their mercy that Kings come closest to gods.

"If he had been as you and you as he, you would have slipped and committed a vice like he did, but he, if he had your position, would not have been as stern and severe as you."

"Please, leave now," Angelo said.

"I wish to Heaven that I had your power," Isabella said, "and that you were me. If that were so, would things be as they are now? No. I would show you what it means to be a judge and what it means to be a prisoner."

Lucio whispered to Isabella, "That's the way to do it! Go after him! Hit him hard with your words!"

"Your brother has forfeited his life because he broke the law," Angelo said. "You are only wasting your words."

"This is evil," Isabella said. "Why, all the souls that have ever existed were forfeited once; Adam committed original sin and sentenced all souls to Hell. Yet God, who could have carried out that sentence, found a way to redeem souls.

"How would you be — what would happen to you when you die — if God, who is the Supreme Judge, should judge you the way that you judge other people? Oh, think about that; and mercy will then breathe within your lips — you will be like a man who has been reborn."

"Restrain yourself, fair maiden," Angelo said. "It is the law, not I, that condemns your brother. Were he my cousin, my brother, or my son, he would still be sentenced to death. He must die tomorrow."

"Tomorrow!" Isabella said. "Oh, that's sudden! That's too quick! Spare him! Spare him! He's not prepared for death. Even for our kitchens we kill the fowl at the right time: after it has been fattened up. Shall we serve Heaven with less respect than we minister to our gross, Earth-bound selves? Shall we send unready souls to be judged? My good, good lord, think about this. Who has died for this offence? Many have committed it."

Lucio whispered to Isabella, "Good point."

"The law has not been dead, although it has slept," Angelo replied. "Those many would not have dared to commit that evil offence, if the first person who disobeyed the law had been punished for his deed. Now that the law is awake, it takes note of what is done; and, like a prophet, it looks into a crystal or into a mirror that shows what future evils, either already newly conceived or soon to be conceived, will be committed because the judges have been remiss in punishing the guilty. These evils that have been in the process of being hatched and born will now have no futures. Before they begin to live, they are dead. The vices are stopped before they are committed."

"Yet show some pity," Isabella said.

"I show pity most of all when I show justice," Angelo replied, "because when I show justice I pity those whom I do not know, people whom an unpunished offence would afterwards gall and harm. A criminal who is not punished will commit the same crime again. I also show pity and do right to an offender who, because he is punished for committing one foul wrong, does not live to commit another foul wrong. Be satisfied and restrain yourself. Your brother dies tomorrow. Reconcile yourself to his death."

"So you must be the first judge who gives this sentence of death, and my brother must be the first who suffers it. Oh, it is excellent to have a giant's strength, but it is tyrannous to use it like a giant. Great power must be wisely used."

Lucio whispered to Isabella, "That's well said."

"If great men could thunder as Jove, the Roman King of the gods, himself does, Jove would never enjoy quiet because every pelting, paltry, insignificant petty officer would fill Jove's Heaven with thunder — nothing but thunder! Merciful Heaven prefers to use the sharp and sulfurous thunderbolt to split the hard, gnarled oak rather than the soft myrtle, but man, proud man, who is dressed in a little and brief authority and who is most ignorant of what he's most assured — the possession of his glassy essence, aka his soul, which mirrors God — acts like an angry ape and plays such fantastic tricks before high Heaven that they make the angels weep, but if the angels had our fallible human nature, they would laugh themselves to death."

Lucio whispered to Isabella, "Stay on the attack! Sic him, girl! He will relent. He's coming round. I know it."

The Provost thought, *Please, Heaven, let Isabella persuade Angelo not to kill Claudio!*

"We cannot regard our brother the way that we regard ourselves," Isabella said. "The great have special privileges. Great men may joke with saints; this shows wit in great men, but if lesser men were to do the same thing, it would be regarded as foul profanation. Great men may also test saints to see if they are truly saintly, but again lesser men cannot do that."

"You are in the right, girl," Lucio whispered to Isabella. "Say more about that; drive the point home."

"If a Captain swears, the Captain is regarded as simply angry," Isabella said, "but if a soldier swears, it is regarded as outright blasphemy."

"Well done," Lucio whispered admiringly to Isabella. "I am surprised that you know such a truth."

"Why are you telling me these things?" Angelo asked.

"Because people in authority, although they err like other people, always have a kind of medicine that will cover up their errors like skin that covers an abscess," Isabella replied. "Go to your bosom and knock there, and ask your heart what it knows that is like my brother's fault. If it confesses to a natural guiltiness such as his, then do not allow your heart to make your tongue pronounce a sentence of death upon my brother. You yourself must have felt the temptation that my brother felt."

Angelo thought, *What Isabella says makes good sense and is true. Her ability to make good sense is actually inflaming me with sexual desire for her. Her good sense is inflaming my senses.*

He said, "Fare you well," and turned to leave.

"My gentle lord, turn back," Isabella requested.

Angelo said, "I will think about what you have said. Come back tomorrow."

This was at least a short reprieve for Claudio. He would not be executed at least until after Angelo and Isabella had talked again.

"Listen to how I will bribe you," Isabella said. "My good lord, turn back."

This mention of a "bribe" surprised and shocked both Angelo and Lucio.

"What!" Angelo said. "Bribe me?"

"Yes, with such gifts that Heaven shall share with you."

Lucio whispered to Isabella, "It is good that you are talking about Heavenly gifts. You would have ruined everything if you did not explain that."

"I will not bribe you with foolish coins made of pure gold," Isabella said, "or with jewels whose value rises or falls with the changes in fashion. I will bribe you with true prayers that shall go up to Heaven and enter there before sunrise. These prayers will come from preserved souls, from fasting maidens whose minds are dedicated to nothing temporal. The nuns in the religious order I will join will pray for you."

"Well," Angelo said. "Come to me tomorrow."

"Good," Lucio whispered to Isabella. "It is well. Let's go now!"

"May Heaven keep your honor safe!" Isabella said to Angelo.

"Amen," Angelo said, and then he thought, *I am heading toward temptation. Isabella's prayer and my prayer are crossed; they are opposite. She prays for my honor to be preserved, but the prayer in my heart is for her honor to become compromised. I want to sleep with her.*

Isabella asked him, "At what hour tomorrow shall I come and talk to your lordship?"

"At any time before noon."

"May God save your honor!" Isabella replied.

Isabella, Lucio, and the Provost left the room.

Angelo, now alone, said to himself, "May God save my honor from you and even from your virtue! What is this? What is happening to me? Is this her fault or mine? Who sins most: the tempter or the tempted? I can't blame her. I can't call her a tempter. This is my fault. I am near her the way that a piece of dead flesh is near a violet. The Sun shines on both the dead flesh and the violet. The violet is nourished, but the dead flesh rots. I do what the dead flesh does: I rot.

"Can it be true that a modest woman may more greatly sexually excite a man than a promiscuous or whorish woman? Is innocence sexually exciting? If we live in an area with a lot of wasteland, should we tear down a sanctuary so that we can build a whorehouse in its place? Plenty of prostitutes are willing to satisfy my sexual desire, so why am I sexually attracted to the chaste Isabella? Damn! Damn! Damn!

"What are you doing, Angelo? Who are you, Angelo? Do you sexually desire Isabella because of those things that make her good and make her a suitable candidate for a sisterhood of nuns?

"Oh, let her brother live! Thieves should go free despite their thefts when judges themselves steal.

"What! Do I love her? Is that why I desire to hear her speak again, and feast upon her eyes? What is it I am dreaming about? Oh, the Devil is a cunning enemy. In order to catch a saint, the Devil baits his hook with a saint! Often, the Devil uses a beautiful woman to entice a man to sin and forfeit his soul!

"The most dangerous temptation is the one that uses our goodness to entice us to sin.

"Never could the strumpet, with all of her duplicitous vigor, cosmetic art, and natural body, even once tempt me to sin, but this virtuous maid has subdued all my virtue.

"Until now, when I saw men who were foolishly infatuated with a woman, I wondered how that was possible."

Duke Vincentio, who was now disguised as a friar, met the Provost.

"Hail to you, Provost!" the disguised Duke Vincentio said. Then, realizing that he was disguised as a friar and was not supposed to personally know the Provost, he added, "At least I think you are the Provost."

"I am the Provost. What do you want, good friar?"

"Bound by my duty to do charity and by my blessed order, I have come to visit the afflicted spirits here in the prison. Grant me the common right of all clerics to see them and tell me the nature of their crimes, so that I may minister to them accordingly."

"I am willing to do more than that, if more is needed," the Provost replied.

Juliet walked over to them.

The Provost said, "Look, here comes one of the prisoners: a gentlewoman in my care, who, falling into a common fault of youth, has blistered her reputation. She is pregnant, and the young man who got her pregnant has been sentenced to death, although he is more suitable to do another such offence and father another child than to die for fathering his first child."

"When must he die?" the disguised Duke Vincentio asked.

"He is sentenced to die tomorrow," the Provost said.

He then said to Juliet, "I have arranged a place for you to give birth. Stay here awhile, and you shall be conducted to that place."

The disguised Duke Vincentio asked Juliet, "Do you repent, fair one, of the sin you carry?"

"I do, and I bear the shame most patiently."

"I'll teach you how to examine your conscience and test your penitence to see if it is sound and genuine, or merely a pretense."

"I'll gladly learn that," Juliet replied.

"Do you love the man who wronged you?" the disguised Duke Vincentio asked.

"Yes, as I love the woman who wronged him. I love him the way that I love myself."

"So then it seems your most offensive act was mutually committed?"

"Yes, mutually."

"Then your sin is of heavier kind than his."

Juliet's sin was literally heavier — her body grew heavier with her pregnancy. Also, she had a heavy burden to bear — she had to carry the fetus in her womb and then give birth to the child.

Some people may think that the woman is more to blame for giving birth outside marriage. Such people think that men always say "Yes," and so it is up to the woman to say "No." However, in their sexist society, men were thought to be more rational than women. Being more rational, men were better able to realize the consequences of their actions and men had the greater responsibility to say "No" to illicit sex.

"I do confess it, and repent it, father," Juliet said.

"It is fitting that you do so, daughter," the disguised Duke Vincentio said, "but perhaps you are repenting because you fear being punished and shamed for your sin. Perhaps you are not repenting because of your love of God. Often, we fear punishment and shame for ourselves, and we do not fear causing pain in Heavenly beings —"

Juliet replied, "I repent because what I did is an evil, and I take the shame with joy. I love the baby whom I will give birth to."

"That is as it should be," the disguised Duke Vincentio said. "Your partner, I hear, has been condemned to die, and I am going to give spiritual instruction to him. May grace go with you. *Benedicite*! May God bless you!"

The disguised Duke Vincentio departed to visit Claudio.

"Claudio must die!" Juliet said. "Love injures me. My life has been spared because I am pregnant, but while I live I will always mourn the horror of Claudio's death."

"Claudio is to be pitied," the Provost said.

In a room of his house, Angelo talked to himself.

"When I want to pray and think, I pray and think on different subjects. Heaven gets my empty words, while my imagination, which does not hear my tongue, anchors and fixates on Isabella. The word 'God' is in my mouth as if I were only mumbling His name. But in my heart is the strong and swelling evil that I have conceived in my imagination.

"The statecraft and political writings that I have studied are like a good thing that has been so often read that it has grown dry and tedious. My dignified solemnity in which — let no man hear me — I take pride I could profitably exchange for the feathered cap of a foolish and foppish courtier. The wind would blow on the feather and make it move and feed the wearer's useless vanity.

"High position and formal manners very often, together with fancy clothing and outward appearance, wrench awe from fools and even influence the wiser souls to believe in your false appearance.

"Appearance and reality need not match. I appear to be good, but what is in my heart now is not good.

"Blood, you are blood. Reality is still reality no matter what appearance suggests.

"Suppose we write the words 'good angel' on the Devil's horns. Despite what is written there, the Devil is not a good angel. My name is Angelo, but what is in my heart is not angelic."

A servant made a noise while entering the room.

Angelo, frightened because of his recognition of the sin in his heart and his thoughts about the Devil, called, "Who's there!"

The servant entered the room and said, "Isabella, a nun, wants to see you."

"Show her the way," Angelo replied.

The servant departed to bring Isabella, who was wearing the clothing of a novice in a nunnery, to Angelo.

Angelo said to himself, "Oh, Heavens! Why does my blood run to my heart, making it unable to function and also depriving all of my other parts of its life-giving functions? It is like way too many soldiers rushing to one place, thereby crowding themselves so much that they are unable to fight and leaving other places undefended.

"Foolish throngs of people do much the same thing when someone faints. They all come to help him, and so they keep from him the air by which he should revive.

"Also similar is when the general public, subjects to a well-liked King, all stop what they are doing and crowd around him in flattering fondness, ignorant of what etiquette requires. Their uncouth love necessarily appears offensive."

Isabella entered the room.

Angelo said, "How are you, fair maiden?"

"I have come to know what you will do about my brother," Isabella said. "I have come to know your pleasure."

"It would much better please me if you knew my pleasure than to demand to know from me what my pleasure is," Angelo said, thinking of his sexual pleasure.

He added, "Your brother cannot live."

"So be it," Isabella said. "May Heaven keep your honor!"

"Yet your brother may live awhile longer, and, perhaps, he may live as long as you or me, but still he must die."

All of us are mortal; we will die at some time.

"You are willing to delay implementing the sentence that requires my brother's death?" Isabella asked.

"Yes."

"Please tell me when his death will happen," Isabella said. "During the reprieve from death, whether the reprieve be long or short, he can take steps to prepare for physical death so that he will not suffer spiritual death. I want his soul to be healthy when his body dies."

"Damn these filthy vices!" Angelo said. "Murder and fornication are equally filthy. A murderer steals a man who has already been made. A fornicator, by creating a pregnancy, creates an illicit image of God, in whose image we are all created. It is as easy to take away the life of a true image of God as it is to create a life that is an illicit and counterfeit image of God. Pardoning the one type of sinner is the same as pardoning the other type of sinner. If I pardon a fornicator, I might as well pardon a murderer."

"It is set down so in Heaven," Isabella said, "but not on Earth. Heaven regards murder and bringing a bastard into the world as equally sins, but we humans on Earth do not."

"Do you think so?" Angelo said. "Then I shall pose to you a question to be answered quickly. Which would you prefer: The very just law now takes your brother's life, or, to redeem him, you give up your body to such sweet uncleanness as the woman has whom he has stained with his lust?"

"Sir, believe this, I prefer to give my body than my soul. I would rather lose my mortal body than my immortal soul."

"I am not talking about your soul. Sins that we are compelled to commit are not truly sins. They are recorded in Heaven's book, but we are not punished for them."

"Do you really believe that?" Isabella asked.

"No, I will not say that I do," Claudio replied. "I can play the Devil's advocate in order to test the people I speak to. I can think of arguments to support both sides. I am trained in law.

"But answer this. I, who am the voice and enforcer of the recorded law, have pronounced a sentence on your brother's life. Might there not be a charity in a sin that would save this brother's life?"

Claudio, of course, was attempting to get Isabella to commit fornication with him in order to save her brother's life. To persuade her, he was trying to make her think of the fornication in this particular situation as being a good deed and a charitable act rather than a sin.

"Please do such a sin," Isabella replied. "I'll swear on my soul that it is no sin at all, but charity."

Isabella was misunderstanding Claudio. She thought the charitable act/sin was pardoning Claudio although he was guilty.

"If you would be willing to do this at the peril of your soul," Claudio said, referring to Isabella committing fornication with him, "sin and charity would be equally balanced."

Isabella again misunderstood Claudio. She thought that he was referring to her begging for her brother's life although her brother was guilty.

Isabella replied, "I do beg for my brother's life. If that is a sin, may Heaven let me bear it!

"I hope that you will grant my suit and pardon my brother. If pardoning my brother is sin, I'll make it my prayer every morning to have it added to my own sins so that the punishment of that sin will not fall on you."

"You are not understanding me," Angelo said. "What you think I am saying is not what I am actually saying. Either you really are ignorant of what I am saying, or you are deliberately appearing to be ignorant of it, and that's not good."

"Let me be ignorant, and let me be in nothing good," Isabella said. "I wish to avoid the sin of pride. I wish to have the divine grace and humility to know I am no better than ignorant and sinful."

"Wisdom wishes to appear brightest when it criticizes itself," Angelo said. "A beauty covered by a black mask has her beauty proclaimed ten times louder than it would be if her beauty were displayed.

"But listen to me. So that you will certainly understand me, I will speak plainly, openly, and bluntly: Your brother is to die."

"That is true."

"And his offence is therefore, so it appears, accountable to the law. That is why he is to die."

"True," Isabella said.

"Let us say that there is no other way to save his life — I am not saying that this is true, or that there exists any way to save his life, but I am postulating it for the sake of argument — except that you, his sister, finding yourself sexually desired by a person who, because of his influence with the judge or because of his own great position in society, could release your brother from the manacles of the all-binding law, and that there were no other Earthly way to save him, but that either you lay down the treasures of your body and give up your virginity to this person, or let your brother die. What would you do?"

"I would do as much for my poor brother as I would do for myself," Isabella replied. "That is, were I sentenced to be beaten and die, the bloody marks left by keen whips I would wear as I would rubies, and I would strip myself to go to my grave as if I were preparing myself to go to my bed that I have been greatly longing for. I would give up my life before I would yield my body up to shame."

"In that case, your brother must die."

"And if he dies, it is the better bargain," Isabella said. "It is better for a brother to die at once, than for a sister, by redeeming him by committing fornication, to die and be damned forever."

"Wouldn't you then be as cruel as the sentence of death that you have so slandered and criticized?"

"Ignominy in ransom and a free pardon without conditions are two different things. Lawful mercy such as a free pardon is not at all like foul redemption — the redemption of one person being dependent upon the sin of another person."

"You seemed recently to consider the law a tyrant, and you seemed to argue that the sliding of your brother into sin was more a frivolous triviality than a vice," Claudio said.

"Pardon me, my lord. It often happens that to get what we want, we do not speak what we really believe. I somewhat did excuse the thing I hate — fornication — in order to help my brother, whom I dearly love, keep his life."

"We are all morally frail," Angelo said.

"If we are not all morally frail, then let my brother die," Isabella replied. "If he is not a mere accomplice among many accomplices, but instead he is the only one who owns and inherits the weakness that you have mentioned, then he should die."

"No, women are morally frail, too," Angelo said.

"Yes, women are as frail as the mirrors where they view themselves, mirrors that are as easily broken as they make reflections of the forms standing in front of them. Women! May Heaven help them! Men, who are created in the image of God, mar their creation and debase themselves when they take advantage of women. Call us women ten times morally frail because we are as soft as our bodies are, and we are susceptible to being seduced and giving birth to illegitimate children."

"I think that what you said is correct," Angelo said. "And from this testimony of your own sex — since I suppose we are made to be not so strong that we cannot be shaken by temptation — let me be bold and say that I believe your own words. Be that which you are — that is, be a woman who is capable of having children. If you are more than a woman, then you are not a woman. But if you are a woman, as your exterior clearly shows that you are, then show that you are a woman now by putting on the destined livery. Wear me and bear me."

Angelo meant that Isabella should embrace him and bear his weight in the missionary position.

"I have no tongue — no language — but one, my gentle lord," Isabella said. "Let me entreat you to speak the language that I speak."

"Plainly conceive, I love you," Angelo said. "Take off your nun's clothing and have sex with me."

"My brother loved Juliet, and you tell me that he shall die because he loved Juliet."

"He shall not die, Isabella, if you give me love and have sex with me."

"I know your virtue has a license in it," Isabella replied. "You can pretend to be fouler than you are in order to uncover the faults of other people. You may be testing me."

"Believe me, on my honor, when I say that my words express my purpose. I am saying exactly what I mean."

"You have little honor although it is widely believed that you have much honor," Isabella said. "What you want is pernicious and wicked. What is good about you is appearance, not reality. I will proclaim to everyone what you really are, Angelo. I mean it. Sign for me an immediate pardon for my brother, or with a wide-open throat I'll shout to the world what kind of man you are."

"Who will believe you, Isabella?" Angelo said. "My name and reputation are unsoiled, my manner of life is austere, and my position in the government is high. I will make a formal statement against you. That and these other things will outweigh your accusation against me. Your own report will choke you, and you will get a reputation for slander. I have begun to feel sexual desire, and now I give my sensuality the rein and let it gallop. Force yourself to consent to my sharp appetite. Set aside all your modesty and your too lengthy blushes; both would have me give up my desire, but both inflame my desire.

"Redeem your brother and save his life by yielding up your body to my lust, or else he must not only die, but your unkindness shall draw out his death — he will be tortured for a long time before he dies.

"Come to me later and give me what I want, or by the passion that now guides me most, I'll prove to be a tyrant to him. As for you, say what you will, my false outweighs your true."

Claudio departed, leaving Isabella alone.

Isabella said to herself, "To whom should I complain? If I were to tell people this, who would believe me? Some mouths are perilous; they bear in them one tongue that condemns at one time and approves at another time the same thing, forcing the law to curtsy to and obey their will. These mouths use their appetite to decide what is right and what is wrong.

"I will go to my brother. Although he has fallen under pressure from his sexual urges, yet he has in him such a mind of honor that, had he twenty heads to put down on twenty bloody blocks so that they can all be cut off, he would yield them up before he would allow his sister to stoop her body to such abhorred pollution. Therefore, Isabella, live chaste, and, brother, die. My chastity is more valuable than my brother. I'll tell him of Angelo's request that I commit fornication, and I will bid him prepare his mind for death and his soul's rest."

CHAPTER 3

— 3.1 —

In a room of the prison, Duke Vincentio, who was still disguised as a friar, talked to Claudio.

Duke Vincentio asked, "So then you are hoping that Lord Angelo will pardon you?"

"The miserable have no other medicine than hope," Claudio replied. "I have hope that I will live, but I am prepared to die."

"Be absolutely sure that you will die," the disguised Duke Vincentio said. "Either death or life — if in fact you are pardoned — shall thereby be the sweeter. Reason thus with life:

"If I lose you, life, I lose a thing that no one but fools would keep.

"Life, you are only a breath, and you are servile to all the skyey astrological influences that hourly afflict this habitation, this body, that you have.

"You, life, are death's fool; you seek to run away from death, but always you are running toward death.

"You, life, are not noble; all the clothing and trappings of civilized existence that you have are nursed by baseness. Human life begins with a baby that dirties its diapers and is completely dependent upon other people, all food is something that was recently alive, magnificent marble architecture begins with blocks of marble cut in a quarry, and the jewels in ornaments were dug from a pit in the ground.

"You, life, are by no means valiant because you fear the soft and tender forked tongue of a poor snake — you are afraid that a venomous bite will kill you. The best of rest is sleep, and sleep is something that living people desire and yet living people are grossly afraid of death, which is no more than a sleep.

"Life, you are not yourself because you exist on many thousands of grains that issue out of dust. Dust a living person used to be, and to dust shall the living person return.

"Life, you are not happy because what you don't have, you always strive to get, and what you do have, you forget and do not value it.

"Life, you are not constant because your mental state alters in strange ways, changing like the Moon.

"Life, if you are rich, you are poor because, like an ass whose back is bowed by heavy gold ingots, you carry your heavy riches during your journey, and your death unloads your riches.

"Life, you have no friends because your own children, who call you their sire, curse the gout, skin disease, and catarrh for not ending your life sooner.

"Life, you have neither youth nor age; instead, it is as if you dream about both while taking a nap after a large lunch. For all of your blessed youth, you are dependent like an old beggar is, and you beg for alms from your old parents who suffer shaking limbs from palsy. And when you are old and rich, you lack the energy, passion, strength, and beauty that would make being rich pleasant.

"Can you call any of this living? More than a thousand additional deaths lie hidden in what we call life, yet we fear death, which makes us all equal."

"I humbly thank you for your words," Claudio said. "To sue to live, I find I seek to die, and, through seeking death, I find life. Therefore, let death come to me."

Isabella came to the door and called, "Hello! May peace be found here, along with grace and good company!"

The Provost said, "Who's there? Come in. Such good wishes deserve a welcome."

The disguised Duke Vincentio said to Claudio, "Dear sir, before long I'll visit you again."

"Most holy sir, I thank you."

Isabella entered the prison cell and said to the Provost, "My business is a word or two with Claudio."

"You are very welcome to talk to him," the Provost said.

He added, "Look, Signior Claudio, here's your sister."

The disguised Duke Vincentio asked, "Provost, may I have a word with you?"

"You may have as many words with me as you please."

The disguised Duke Vincentio whispered, "I wish to overhear their conversation. Take me to a concealed place where I can overhear them."

Duke Vincentio was disguised as a friar, and the Provost was willing to conceal the friar — and would have been willing to conceal Duke Vincentio if he had known the friar's true identity.

The disguised Duke Vincentio and the Provost left.

"Now, sister, what's the comfort you bring me?" Claudio asked.

"Why, as all comforts are, it is very good, very good indeed. Lord Angelo, having business in Heaven, intends to swiftly make you his permanent ambassador in Heaven. Therefore make your best preparations speedily; tomorrow you go to Heaven."

"Is there no remedy?"

"None, except for a remedy that, to save a head, would cut a heart in two and cause extreme anguish."

"But is there any remedy?"

"Yes, brother, it is possible for you to live. There is a Devilish mercy in the judge, that if you'll implore it, it will free your life, but fetter you until death."

"Perpetual durance?"

Claudio meant life in prison, but Isabella interpreted his phrase as meaning perpetual guilt.

"Yes, just exactly that: perpetual durance, a restraint. Even if you were free to travel throughout the world, you would still be restrained."

Isabella meant that Claudio would not be able to escape from his guilt no matter where he traveled.

"What kind of restraint?" Claudio asked.

"Such a one as, if you consented to it, would tear your honor away from you just like bark being stripped from a tree. You would be left naked, without honor."

"Let me know the point. Speak clearly."

"I am afraid of what you may decide, Claudio; and I quake in fear that you would value a feverous life and more greatly respect six or seven additional winters than an everlasting honor. Do you dare to die?

"The feeling we have in death is mostly fearful anticipation rather than pain. The poor beetle, which we tread upon, in bodily suffering endures a pang of pain as great as when a giant dies."

Isabella meant that the suffering during death of a giant was no worse than the suffering of a beetle that is stepped on; however, her words could be interpreted as saying that the suffering during death of a beetle was as great as the suffering of a dying giant. Her words could also be interpreted as saying that all creatures, great and small, fear death, suffer during death, and want to keep on living.

"Why are you trying to make me feel shame?" Claudio asked. "Do you think that your flowery words of tenderness can make me resolve to die? Do I need your flowery words to reconcile myself to death? If I must die, I will encounter darkness as I would a bride, and hug it in my arms."

"There spoke my brother; when you said those words a voice metaphorically came out of my father's grave," Isabella said. "Yes, you must die: You are too noble to save your life with dishonorable expedients.

"Angelo is a deputy who outwardly appears to be a saint. His grave visage is immovable and his deliberate words nip youth in the head the way that a falcon bites its prey to kill it. He also drives follies into hiding the way that a falcon does a fowl. Nevertheless, Angelo is a Devil. If his sin were to be vomited out of him the way that mud and silt are removed from a pond, his sin would appear to fill a pond as deep as hell."

"The gilted Angelo!" Claudio cried.

"Oh, hypocrisy is the cunning uniform of Hell, which invests and covers the damnedest body in gilted trimmings! Hell can give a damned soul the appearance of a Puritan!

"Claudio, what do you think about this? If I were to give Angelo my virginity, he would set you free."

"Oh, Heavens! That cannot be true," Claudio said.

"Yes, it is true," Isabella replied. "He would give to you — in return for this rank offence, this sexual harassment and intended rape of me — the freedom to continue to offend him. He would allow you to continue to sin with Juliet.

"This night is the time when I should do what I abhor to name, or else you die."

"Don't do it," Claudio said.

"If he wanted my life, I would throw it down for your deliverance from death as readily as I would throw away a pin."

"Thanks, dear Isabella."

"Be ready, Claudio, for your death tomorrow. Be prepared to die."

"Yes," Claudio said.

He immediately began to have second thoughts.

He asked, "Has Angelo sexual desires in him that thus can make him bite the law on the nose and treat it with contempt, when he should instead enforce the law? Surely, it is no sin, or of the seven deadly sins, it is the least sinful sin."

"Which is the least?"

"If lechery were damnable, and with Angelo being so wise, why would he for a short bout of sex and folly be everlastingly punished in Hell? Oh, Isabella!"

"What are you saying!"

"Death is a thing to be feared."

"And a shamed life is to be hated."

"Yes, but to die, and go we know not where; to lie trapped in a cold corpse and to rot; to have this alert and warm body become a clod of clay, to have this spirit, which is capable of feeling delight, bathe in fiery floods or reside in a piercingly cold region of thickly layered ice; to be imprisoned in the invisible winds and blown with restless violence round about a world that is suspended in space; or to be worse than the worst of those souls whom unrestrained and uncertain thought imagine to be howling in Hell: It is too horrible!

"The weariest and most loathed worldly life that age, aches and pains of every bodily kind, penury, and imprisonment can lay on us in the Land of the Living is a paradise to what we fear we will endure when we are dead."

"I can't believe what I am hearing!"

"Sweet sister, let me live," Claudio pleaded. "What sin you do to save a brother's life, our sibling love for each other will make so much allowance for the deed that it will become a virtue."

"Oh, you beast without a moral sense! Oh, you faithless coward! Oh, you dishonest wretch! Will you be made a man out of — be given life because of — my vice?

"Isn't it a kind of incest, to take life from your own sister's shame? From my illicit sex you would be 'reborn and come to life' again! What should I think about you?

"Heaven forbid my mother played my father fair and was faithful to him! My father never fathered such a warped and wild weed as you! You must be a bastard! I defy you! You are no brother of mine! Die! Perish! If I could stop your death simply by bending down, I would not! I would let you die! I'll pray a thousand prayers that you die; I will not pray a single word to save you."

"Please, listen to me, Isabella."

"Your sin is not a one-time occurrence; it is your career, your habitual way of life. Showing mercy to you would simply allow you to commit more fornication. It is best that you die quickly."

"Please, listen to me, Isabella."

Duke Vincentio, still disguised as a friar, had heard every word. Now he came out of hiding and said to Isabella, "Allow me to say a word, young sister — only one word."

"What do you want?"

"If you will give me some of your leisure time, I want to speak with you soon. What I would ask from you is something that will benefit you."

"I have no superfluous leisure time," Isabella replied. "The time that I spend with you is time that must be stolen from the other things that I need to do, but I will talk to you for a while."

She walked a short distance away, and so she was unable to hear Duke Vincentio talk to Claudio, her brother.

The disguised Duke Vincentio said, "Son, I have overheard the conversation that has passed between you and your sister. Angelo never intended to corrupt her; he only made a test of her virtue to see if his judgment of people's characters was correct. She, having the integrity of honor in her, made him that virtuous denial that he was very glad to receive. I am confessor to Angelo, and I know this to be true; therefore, prepare to die. Do not comfort yourself with false hopes. Tomorrow you must die; get on your knees, pray, and get ready to die."

"Let me ask my sister to pardon me," Claudio said. "I am so out of love with life that I would beg to be rid of it."

"Keep that thought. Farewell."

Claudio went to his sister, talked briefly with her, and left the room.

As Claudio and Isabella were talking, the disguised Duke Vincentio said, "Provost, may I have a word with you?"

The Provost came forward and asked, "What do you want, father?"

"That now you have come here, you will leave. Leave me alone for a while with the maiden Isabella. My mind and my friar's robe both proclaim that I intend no harm to her. She shall not be harmed while she is alone with me."

"Very well," the Provost said, and then he left the room.

Isabella came over to the disguised Duke Vincentio, who said to her, "The hand that has made you beautiful has made you good. Beauty often discards goodness — beauty and chastity seldom meet. But because grace is the soul of your character, you will always be beautiful and virtuous.

"Fortune and luck have made known to me the assault on your virtue that Angelo has made; and, except that I know of other examples of Angelo's sinfulness, I should wonder at Angelo. What will you do to content this deputy for Duke Vincentio — Angelo — and to save your brother?"

"I am going to Angelo now to tell him what I have decided," Isabella replied. "I prefer that my brother die by the law than that my son should be a bastard — unlawfully born. But how greatly is good Duke Vincentio deceived in Angelo! If ever he returns and I can speak to him, I will open my lips in vain, or I will reveal Angelo's sinful conduct."

"That should be a good thing to do," the disguised Duke Vincentio said, "yet, as the matter now stands, he will avoid your accusation; he will say that he was only making trial of you and testing your virtue. Therefore listen to what I advise. I want to help, and I have an idea that can make all things right.

"I believe that you may very righteously do a poor wronged lady a benefit that she deserves, redeem your brother from the angry law and prevent his death, do no stain of sin to your own gracious person, and much please the absent Duke Vincentio if he ever returns and hears about this business."

"Let me hear you speak more about your plan," Isabella said. "I have the courage to do anything that appears to be not foul and sinful to me."

"Virtue is bold, and goodness is never fearful," the disguised Duke Vincentio said. "Have you heard of Mariana, the sister of Frederick, the great soldier who drowned at sea?"

"I have heard of the lady, and good words went with her name. She has a good reputation."

"Angelo should have married her; he was engaged by oath to marry her. With such an oath, many couples have sex. When sex occurs, a wedding is mandatory. If sex does not occur, then in some situations, such as the unfaithfulness of one partner, the engagement can be lawfully and ethically broken. The wedding day of Angelo and Mariana was set, but between the time of the engagement and the wedding Frederick, Mariana's brother, was wrecked at sea. The ship was carrying Mariana's dowry.

"Listen to the bad things that befell the poor gentlewoman. She lost a noble and renowned brother, who in his love toward her was always most kind and brotherly. Along with him, she lost the greatest part of her fortune: her marriage-dowry. She also lost her husband-to-be: this Angelo who has the reputation of being so virtuous."

"Can this be true?" Isabella asked. "Did Angelo leave her?"

"He left her in her tears, and he did not dry one of them with his comfort. He swallowed his vows to her whole and did not keep them; instead, he pretended that she had been unfaithful to him.

"In short, Angelo bestowed on her what was already hers: her own lamentation. Even now, she weeps for him, and her tears affect him the way they would marble — not at all."

"Death would deserve much praise if it were to take this poor virgin Mariana from the world! What corruption is in this life, that it will let this man Angelo continue to live! But how can she receive any benefit from this situation?"

"You may easily heal the rupture between Angelo and Mariana. By doing so, you will save your brother, and you will do so without losing any honor."

"Tell me how I can do this, good father."

"The virgin Mariana still loves Angelo; his unjust unkindness that in all reason should have quenched her love for him has, like an obstacle or impediment in a current of water, made it more violent and unruly.

"Go to Angelo; answer his sexual harassment of you with a plausible obedience," the disguised Duke Vincentio said. "Agree with his demands and say that you will sleep with him, but with conditions. First, your stay with him must not be long. Second, the time must be dark and silent, with no one bustling about. Third, the place must be convenient for you.

"This being granted — now comes the most important part — we shall advise this wronged maiden to go to the appointment instead of you. She will go in your place; if the sexual encounter becomes public afterward, it may compel Angelo to marry her. If this plan works, your brother will be saved, your honor remain untainted, the poor Mariana advantaged by being married, and the corrupt deputy weighed in the scales of justice.

"I will go to the maiden Mariana and inform her of our plan and prepare her for the sexual encounter with Angelo.

"If you agree to participate in carrying out his plan, the benefits will justify the deceit. The benefits will be a shield against reproof.

"What do you think?"

Isabella replied, "The plan itself makes me happy, and I trust the plan will result in a very prosperous and perfect outcome."

"It depends very much on your being able to do your part of the plan," the disguised Duke Vincentio said. "Go speedily to Angelo. If he wants you to go to his bed tonight, say that you agree. I will go immediately to Saint Luke's. There, at a farmhouse surrounded by a ditch resides this dejected Mariana. At that place come and see me and tell me what happened when you met with Angelo. Meet with Angelo quickly, so that you can visit me soon."

"I thank you for this comfort," Isabella said. "Fare you well, good father."

She departed.

Several people entered the room in which the disguised Duke Vincentio was standing: Elbow the Constable, Pompey the part-time pimp, and some law-enforcement officers.

Elbow said to Pompey, "Unless we can stop you pimps from buying and selling men and women like beasts, we shall see female bellies all over the world filled with brown and white bastard — and I don't mean just the wine we call 'bastard.'"

The disguised Duke Vincentio thought, *Heavens! What is going on here?*

Pompey replied, "The world has two usuries: prostitution and usury. Prostitution creates bastards; usury creates interest. It has not been a merry world since the practitioners of the merrier usury — prostitution — were outlawed and prosecuted, and practitioners of the worse usury — lending money at high interest — were encouraged by order of law to grow rich and wear expensive clothing such as a furred gown to keep each usurer warm. The furs were fox on top of lamb, to signify craftiness overcoming innocence, and to signify that craft, being richer than innocence, is more important and highly regarded in this world."

"Come this way, sir," Elbow said to Pompey.

Then he said to Duke Vincentio, who was still disguised as a friar, "Bless you, good father friar."

"And bless you, good brother father."

"Father" was a term used in their society to refer to an older man as well as to a priest; Elbow was an older man.

The disguised Duke Vincentio continued: "What offence has this man committed, sir? What has he done to offend you?"

"Sir, he has offended the law," Elbow replied, "and, sir, we think that he is a thief, too, sir, because we have found upon him, sir, a strange picklock, which we have sent to the deputy."

The picklock was a skeleton key that was used to unlock many doors.

Hearing this, the disguised Duke Vincentio was able to guess Pompey's occupation.

"Heavens!" he said to Pompey. "You are a bawd, a wicked bawd! You are a pimp! The evil that you have caused to be done, that is the means by which you live. Do you ever think what it means to cram your mouth with food or clothe your back from such a filthy vice? Do you ever say to yourself, 'From their abominable and beastly sexual touches I drink, I eat, I clothe myself, and I live?' Can you believe that you are living a good life when its maintenance depends on such a stinking business? Mend your life! Sin no more!"

Pompey replied, "Indeed, it does stink in some ways, sir, but yet, sir, I would argue —"

"No, if the Devil has given you arguments in favor of sin, you will show that you are the Devil's property," the disguised Duke Vincentio said.

He then said to Elbow, "Take him to prison, officer: Punishment and instruction must both do their work before this rude beast will learn to mend his ways."

"He must appear before Angelo, the Duke's deputy, sir," Elbow replied. "Angelo has given Pompey warning: The deputy cannot abide a whoremaster. If anyone is a whoremonger and appears before Angelo, it would be better if he were to do anything else but appear before Angelo."

The disguised Duke Vincentio was able to recognize that Pompey had at least one good characteristic: He was not a hypocrite.

The disguised Duke Vincentio thought, *I wish that we were all as free from sin as Angelo falsely seems to be, and as free from hypocrisy as Pompey actually is.*

Elbow said about Pompey, "His neck will come to your waist — a cord, sir."

Elbow was referring to the cord, aka rope, that Duke Vincentio wore around his waist because he was disguised as a friar. Pompey's neck would be in a noose if he were punished for his crime by being hung.

Seeing Lucio coming toward them, Pompey said, "I spy comfort; I see money for my bail. Here's a gentleman and a friend of mine."

Lucio said, "How are you, noble Pompey! What, at the wheels of Caesar? Are you being led in triumph?"

In Roman triumphs, defeated enemies would walk behind the vehicle that carried their conqueror. In history, Pompey was never led in triumph. However, his sons were led in triumph after Julius Caesar defeated them in 45 B.C.E. in the Battle of Munda.

Lucio continued: "What, is there none of Pygmalion's images, a newly made woman, to be had now by putting one's hand in one's pocket and extracting it clutched?"

Pygmalion was an ancient sculptor who fell in love with one of his statues: that of a lovely young woman. He prayed to Aphrodite, goddess of sexual desire, who brought the statue to life. Pygmalion married the newly created woman and together they had a son.

In their society, statues were often painted, and prostitutes in his society used paint — makeup; therefore, when Lucio referred to Pygmalion's images, he was referring to prostitutes. Men would reach into their pockets, clutch money, and pull the money out in order to pay for the prostitute.

Lucio asked Pompey, "Do you have anything to say in reply? Huh? What do you have to say to this tune, matter, and method? Has a flood washed away sin? What do you have to say, mate? How do you like Angelo's reforms? Is your way of life completely destroyed? Are you unhappy? Are you unable to speak? How is it going for you?"

The disguised Duke Vincentio thought, *He babbles and babbles, and then he babbles worse than before!*

"How is my dear morsel, your mistress? Does Mistress Overdone still work as a procurer?"

"Indeed, sir," Pompey said, "she has eaten up all her beef, and she is herself in the tub."

Beef was slang for flesh-food that had been prepared for consumption — or, more simply, prostitutes. A treatment for venereal disease was to sweat in a tub. Tubs were also used to salt, aka powder, beef.

"Why, this is good," Lucio replied. "This is the right of it; it must be so. A fresh whore must become a powdered bawd — it is inevitable. Are you going to prison, Pompey?"

"Yes, indeed, sir."

"Why, it is not amiss, Pompey," Lucio said. "It is hardly a surprise. Farewell. Go, and say that I sent you there. Are you going to prison for debt, Pompey? Or for what reason?"

Lucio had a cruel streak in him. He knew why Pompey was going to prison. In fact, he may have informed on Pompey and on Mistress Overdone.

"I am going to prison for being a bawd," Pompey replied.

Lucio said to Elbow, "Well, then, imprison him. If imprisonment is the due of a bawd, why, it is his right to be in prison. He is without doubt a bawd, and from antiquity, too. He was bawd-born — given birth by a bawd, and born to be a bawd."

Lucio added, "Farewell, good Pompey. Commend me to the prison, Pompey. You will act like a good husband now, Pompey; you will stay at home in your house."

"I hope, sir, your good worship will pay my bail," Pompey said.

"No, indeed, I will not pay your bail, Pompey; it is not the fashion these days to pay the bail of bawds. Instead, I will pray, Pompey, to increase your bondage, your time in prison. That is the fashion nowadays. If you do not take your time patiently, why, your mettle, aka spirit, is all the more — as will be the metal of your fetters. *Adieu*, trusty Pompey."

Lucio then said to the disguised Duke Vincentio, "Bless you, friar."

"And you," the disguised Duke Vincentio replied.

"Does Bridget still paint, Pompey? Does she still wear makeup?" Lucio asked.

Elbow said to Pompey, "Come this way, sir."

"You will not pay my bail, then, sir?" Pompey asked Lucio.

"No, Pompey, not then and not now," Lucio replied.

He then asked, "What is the news, friar? What is the news?"

Elbow repeated, "Come this way, sir. Come."

"Go to your kennel, Pompey," Lucio said. "Go."

Elbow, Pompey, and the officers departed, leaving Lucio and the disguised Duke Vincentio alone.

"What news, friar, have you heard about the Duke?"

"I have heard none. Can you tell me of any?"

"Some say that he is with the Emperor of Russia; others say that he is in Rome. But where do you think he is?"

"I don't know where he is, but wherever he is, I wish him well."

"It was a mad and eccentric trick of him to steal secretly away from Vienna and usurp the beggary he was never born to. He left his high position here, and wherever he is, he has a lower position than ruler. Lord Angelo dukes it well in his absence; he severely punishes criminals."

"He does well when it comes to punishment."

"A little more leniency when it comes to lechery would do no harm in him; he is somewhat too crabbed that way, friar."

"It is too prevalent a vice, and severity must cure it."

"Yes, truly the vice is prevalent. It has many partakers and many friends, and it is impossible to stop until eating and drinking have been stopped. When there are no more people, there will be no more lechery.

"They say that this Angelo was not made by man and woman in the usual way of producing children. Is it true, do you think?" Lucio asked.

"How else could he have been made, then?"

"Some say that a sea-maid, aka mermaid, spawned him; some say that he was begotten by two dried codfishes. But it is certain that when he makes water, aka pees, his urine is hard pellets of ice — that I know to be true. He also has the reproductive capacity of a puppet — there can be no doubt about that."

"You are full of jokes, sir, and speak rapidly," the disguised Duke Vincentio said, and then he thought, *You speak so rapidly that you speak without thinking.*

"Why, Angelo is ruthless — he is willing to take away the life of a man because of the criminal rebellion of what the man has in between his legs! Would the Duke who is absent have done this? Before he would have hanged a man for begetting a hundred bastards, the Duke would have paid for the nursing of a thousand bastards. The Duke had some feeling for the act of sex: He knew the service and utility of it, and that taught him to be merciful."

"I never heard that the absent Duke had much of a reputation for sleeping with women; he was not inclined to engage in unethical sex."

"Oh, sir, you are deceived," Lucio said. "You are wrong."

"It is not possible."

"You don't believe that the Duke was inclined to engage in unethical sex? Yes, he was. When he saw a beggar who was fifty years old, he used to put a ducat in her dish, if you know what I mean and I think you do. The Duke had strange fancies in him. He used to be drunk, too — I can tell you that."

"You do him wrong, surely," the disguised Duke Vincentio said.

"Sir, I was an intimate friend of his. A sly fellow was the Duke, and I believe I know the cause of his leaving Vienna."

"What, I ask, might be the cause?"

"No, you must pardon me for not telling you," Lucio said. "It is a secret that must be locked within my teeth and lips, but I can tell you this: The majority of his subjects believe that the Duke is wise."

"Wise! Why, there is no question but that the Duke is in fact wise!"

"He is a very superficial, ignorant, unweighing fellow," Lucio said.

"Either this is envy in you, or folly, or a mistake," the disguised Duke Vincentio said. "The very stream of his life and his management of Vienna must — if a reference were needed — give him a better proclamation. His biography and the record of his rule in Vienna show him to be much better than what you have said about him. Let his achievements testify for him, and he shall appear even to the envious to be a scholar, a statesman, and a soldier. Therefore you speak ignorantly and without knowledge, or if you have some knowledge of the Duke, you have much darkened your evaluation of the Duke because of malice toward him."

"Sir, I know him, and I love him," Lucio said, falsely. He did not know Duke Vincentio.

"Love talks with better knowledge, and knowledge with dearer love. Someone who loved the Duke would know him better than you do, and someone who knew the Duke would love him more than you do."

"Come, sir, I know what I know."

"I can hardly believe that, since you don't know what you are saying. But, if the Duke ever did return, as our prayers are that he will, let me desire you to make your charges in his presence. If you have spoken the truth, you will have the courage to maintain that it is the truth. I am bound by duty to summon you to testify before the Duke that what you have said about him is true, and so I ask you for your name."

"Sir, my name is Lucio; my name is well known to the Duke."

"He shall know you better, sir, if I may live to report to him what you have said about him."

"I am not afraid of you."

"Oh, you hope that the Duke will not return to Vienna, or you imagine that I am someone who cannot hurt you. But indeed I can do you little harm: You will swear before the Duke that you did not say these things."

"I'll be hanged first," Lucio said. "You are deceived about me, friar. But no more about this. Can you tell me whether Claudio is to die or not?"

"Why should Claudio die, sir?"

"Why? For filling a bottle with a funnel, if you know what I mean and I think you do. I wish that the Duke we have been talking about would return to Vienna again. This deputy without genitals will depopulate the province with continence and abstinence from sex. He will not allow sparrows to build nests in his house eaves because sparrows are lecherous. The Duke always would have dark deeds darkly answered; he would never bring them to light. Since no one was ever charged with crimes of lechery, the crimes were never punished. I wish that the Duke would return! This Claudio is condemned to death because he took off his pants. Farewell, good friar. Please, pray for me. The Duke, I say to you again, would eat mutton on Fridays."

Fridays were days of abstinence from meat for Catholics, and Lucio was saying that Duke Vincentio would eat meat on days of abstinence. And since "mutton" was a slang word for prostitutes, Lucio was saying that Duke Vincentio would engage in illicit sex.

Lucio added, "He's now past fornication because of old age, yet even now I say to you that he would kiss a beggar even if she smelt of brown bread and garlic. Say that I said so. Farewell."

Lucio exited, and the disguised Duke Vincentio said to himself, "No powerful or great people can escape censure; back-biting calumny will strike at the whitest virtue. What King is so strong that he can tie up the gall in a slanderous tongue? But who is coming here?"

Escalus, the Provost, and some law-enforcement officers entered the room. With them was Mistress Overdone, who had been arrested.

Escalus said, "Go and take her away to her prison cell!"

"My good lord, be good to me," Mistress Overdone pleaded. "Your honor has the reputation of being a merciful man, my good lord."

"You have been warned two and three times, and yet you are again guilty of the same crime!" Escalus said. "This would make even the embodiment of Mercy swear and play the tyrant by giving you a harsh sentence."

The Provost said, "She has been a bawd for eleven years' continuance, may it please your honor."

Of course, such information would not please Escalus, but "may it please your honor" was an idiom meaning "if your honor doesn't mind my telling you."

Mistress Overdone said, "My lord, this information against me comes from Lucio. He made Mistress Kate Keepdown pregnant when the Duke was still in Vienna. Lucio promised to marry her. His child is a year and a quarter old, come the feast day of Saint Philip and Saint Jacob: May 1. I myself have taken care of his child, and see how he goes around and abuses me!"

"Lucio is a fellow who frequently disregards the law," Escalus said. "Let him be brought before us. Take her to her prison cell!"

Mistress Overdone wanted to plead with Escalus, but he told her, "Don't. No more words."

The law-enforcement officers took Mistress Overdone away.

Escalus said, "Provost, my colleague Angelo will not change his mind: Claudio must die. Let him be provided with religious advisors and all charitable preparation that Christians can provide. If Angelo administered justice with the amount of pity that I feel for Claudio, Claudio would not be going to die."

"If you don't mind my saying so," the Provost said, "this friar has been with Claudio, and he has given him spiritual counsel to help him accept his death."

"Good day, good father," Escalus said.

"May blessings and goodness fall upon you!" the disguised Duke Vincentio said.

"Where are you from?"

"I am not from this country, although now I am able to reside here for a while. I am a brother of a gracious order, recently come from the Holy See on special business from his holiness."

"What news is abroad in the world?" Escalus asked.

The answer given by the disguised Duke Vincentio was bitter and cynical: "None, except that so great a fever is afflicting goodness that only the death of goodness can cure the fever.

"The only things in demand in the modern world are the newest things — newness for its own sake. Obviously, we should make use of the old things that work, and we should replace them with new things only when the new things work better.

"To be aged in any undertaking is considered to be as dangerous as it is considered virtuous to be faithful in any undertaking. Obviously, it ought to be considered a virtue to be faithful only to *good* undertakings. Obviously, one should become aged only as a result of working on *good* undertakings. These days, to be virtuous is to be in danger.

"Scarcely enough trustworthiness is in existence to make societies secure and make it safe to associate with other people, but there is foolish optimism enough to make many 'friendships' cursed because pretend friends will take advantage of the foolish optimists. Obviously, things work out best if everyone is true to their word and no one takes advantage of another person.

"The wisdom of the world considers and thinks about these riddling problems.

"This news is old enough, we have heard it before, and yet it is news that we hear again every day."

The disguised Duke Vincentio hesitated and then asked, "Please, sir, tell me what kind of disposition did the absent Duke have?"

Escalus replied, "He was one who, above all other battles, fought especially to know himself. He did his best to follow this ancient piece of wisdom: Know thyself."

"What kind of pleasure did he enjoy?"

"He preferred to rejoice at seeing another person being merry rather than himself be merry; he was a gentleman of all temperance," Escalus said. "But let's not talk about him, but simply pray that his business may prove to be prosperous; instead, tell me about Claudio. Is he prepared to die? I understand that you have visited him."

"Claudio does not believe that he has received an unjust sentence from his judge. He most willingly humbles himself and accepts his sentence; however, his human weakness had led him to imagine possible scenarios in which he would not lose his life. I have spent time with him and let him know that none of these futile hopes has any basis in reality, and now he knows that he will die."

"You have done your duty to Heaven and to the prisoner," Escalus said. "I have labored to get a lesser sentence for the poor gentleman to the furthest limit of my humble ability, but Angelo is so severe in giving sentences that he has forced me to tell him that he is indeed acting like the embodiment of Justice. By that, I mean he is the embodiment of Justice without Mercy."

"If his own life is as virtuous as he wants and expects other people to be, it is well for him, but if he fails to live up to the standards that he imposes on other people, he has sentenced himself — he shall receive the same punishment that he gives to other people," Duke Vincentio, still disguised as a friar, said. "So it is written in Matthew 7:2: 'For with what judgment ye judge, ye shall be judged: and with what measure ye mete, it shall be measured to you again.'"

"I am going to visit the prisoner," Escalus said. "Fare you well."

"May peace be with you!"

Alone, the disguised Duke Vincentio said to himself, "He who the sword of Heaven — judicial power — will bear should be as holy as severe; he must be holy if he gives severe sentences. He must know that he is to set a good example for others to follow. He must have the grace to stand firmly on his principles, and he must have the strength to act upon them. He must not judge other people more harshly or less harshly than he judges himself. May the judge be shamed who gives the death sentence to people who commit crimes and sins that the judge himself commits and enjoys! May Angelo be twice treble shamed because he weeds my vice — which was to allow for a long time some sexual crimes to go unpunished — and lets his own vices grow!

"Oh, what vices may a man hide within him although he appears to be an angel on the outward side! The man has committed the same crimes as other people but deceived everyone by hiding his crimes. He uses worthless spiders' strings to drag the most ponderous and substantial things to a place of shame! His hypocrisy shames his supposed virtue.

"I must apply craft against vice. With Angelo tonight shall sleep Mariana, whom he once betrothed but now despises, and so the disguised Mariana will pay Angelo what he demands from Isabella. She will pay him with falsehood — the illusion that she is Isabella. By so paying him, Mariana will fulfill the old pre-marriage contract that she and Angelo had made — with the result that Angelo *must* marry her."

CHAPTER 4

— 4.1 —

Mariana and a boy were outside the farmhouse at St. Luke's. She listened as the boy sang this song:

"*Take, oh, take those lips away,*

"*That so sweetly were forsworn;*

"*And those eyes, the break of day,*

"*Lights that do mislead the morn —*

"*They are eyes so bright that the morning mistakes them for the rising Sun.*

"*But my kisses bring again, bring again,*

"*Seals of love — kisses — but sealed in vain, sealed in vain.*"

The theme of the song was a false vow of love.

"Stop singing," Mariana, who saw the disguised Duke Vincentio coming toward them, said to the boy. "Quickly go away. I see coming here a man of comfort, whose advice has often quieted my troublesome discontent."

The boy departed.

Mariana said to the disguised Duke Vincentio, "Please pardon me, sir. I well wish that you had not found me here listening to music. Let me excuse myself. Please believe me when I say that the music did not amuse me with unseemly merriment but it did soothe my sorrow."

"That is good," the disguised Duke Vincentio said, "although music often has such a charm that it can make sin seem to be good, and lead good to what can harm it.

"Please, tell me whether anybody has inquired for me here today. I have promised to meet someone here just about this time."

"No one has been here seeking you. I have sat here all day," Mariana said.

Isabella now walked toward them.

"I always believe what you say," the disguised Duke Vincentio said. "The person I was going to meet has just shown up. Now I want you to leave us alone for a little while. I hope to let you know very soon about something that will bring some advantage to yourself."

"I am always bound to you and will obey you," Mariana said as she exited.

The disguised Duke Vincentio said to Isabella, "We are very well met, and you have well come at a welcome time. What is the news that you bring me from this good deputy?"

"He has a garden surrounded with a brick wall, whose western side has a vineyard. Leading into that vineyard is a gate made of wooden planks. I have two keys. The bigger key will open that gate. The smaller key opens a little door that from the vineyard leads to the garden. I have promised to visit Angelo at the garden house during the drowsy middle of the night."

"Do you have the knowledge that is needed to find this way and reach Angelo?"

"I have carefully noted and memorized the way," Isabella replied. "Angelo whispered guiltily to me twice how to find the way there although he did not show me the way."

"Is there anything else — such as a password — that you two have agreed upon that Mariana ought to know?"

"No, none," Isabella replied. "We have agreed that the tryst should take place in the dark. I also told him that 'my' stay must necessarily be brief because, I said, I have a servant who will come along with me and wait for me. I said that this servant believes that I am visiting Angelo to talk to him about my brother."

"This is well thought out," the disguised Duke Vincentio said. "I have not yet made known to Mariana a word of this. So far, she knows nothing about our plan."

He called, "Mariana, come here!"

Mariana walked toward the two.

The disguised Duke Vincentio said to her, "Please, become acquainted with this maiden. She has come here to do something good for you."

"What he said is true," Isabella said.

The disguised Duke Vincentio said to Mariana, "Do you believe that I respect you and want to do good things for you?"

"Good friar, I know you do," Mariana said. "I have always found that to be true."

"Take, then, this woman, your new companion, by the hand. She has something to tell you. I will soon talk to you. Be quick; the damp nighttime is coming."

Mariana asked Isabella, "Is it OK if we talk over here?"

They withdrew a short distance away and talked.

The disguised Duke Vincentio said to himself, "Oh, people in high and great positions! Millions of evil eyes stare at you. Volumes of voices speak false and antagonistic things about your actions the way that a pack of dogs howl while following a false trail. A thousand foolish wits make you the subjects of their daydreams in which they stretch you on the rack."

Mariana and Isabella had finished their conversation.

"Welcome," the disguised Duke Vincentio said. "Is there an agreement to follow this plan?"

"Mariana will take the enterprise upon her, father," Isabella said, "if you advise it."

"I do advise it, and I also urge you, Mariana, to do this."

Isabella said to Mariana, "You have little to say. When you depart from him, say, softly and lowly, 'Remember now my brother.'"

"Do not fear," Mariana said. "I will remember to say it."

"And, gentle daughter, don't you fear anything at all," the disguised Duke Vincentio said. "Angelo is your husband on a pre-contract of marriage. To bring you together like this is no sin because the justice of your title to him outweighs the deceit.

"Come, let all of us go. Our corn's yet to reap, for our seed's yet to sow. We have much more to do before we can reap the harvest of our plan."

The Provost and Pompey talked together in the prison.

"Come here," the Provost said to Pompey. "Can you cut off a man's head?"

"If the man is a bachelor, sir, I can, but if he is a married man, he is his wife's head, and I could never cut off a woman's head."

Pompey was referring to Ephesians 5:23: "For the husband is the wife's head, even as Christ is the head of the Church, and the same is the Savior of his body."

"Come, sir, set aside your quibbles, and give me a direct answer," the Provost said. "This morning Claudio and Barnardine are scheduled to die. Here is in our prison a common executioner, who in his job lacks a helper. If you will take it on yourself to assist him, it shall free you from your fetters; if not, you shall serve your full time of imprisonment and then you will be set free with a pitiless whipping, for you have been a notorious bawd."

"Sir, I have been an unlawful bawd for longer than I can remember, but yet I will be content to be a lawful hangman. I would be glad to receive some instruction from my fellow partner."

The Provost called the common executioner: "Abhorson! Where's Abhorson?"

Abhorson, whose name combined the words "abhor" and "whoreson," aka son of a whore, entered the room and asked, "Are you calling for me, sir?"

"Here's a fellow who will help you tomorrow in your executions. If you think it suitable, make an agreement to employ him for the next year, and let him stay here with you. If you do not think it suitable, use him for the present and then dismiss him. Because he has been a bawd, he cannot plead that he is too good to be an executioner."

"A bawd, sir? Damn him! He will discredit our mystery. He will discredit our skilled labor."

In their society, "mystery" meant "skilled labor." How to do the labor was a mystery to those who had not acquired the skills necessary to do it.

"Come on," the Provost said. "Being an executioner and being a bawd have the same status — they weigh the same, and it takes a feather to make one side of the scales sink."

The Provost exited.

Pompey said, "Please, sir, give me your good favor — and I am sure that you have good favor, although you have a hangdog look. Sir, do you call your occupation a mystery?"

"Yes, sir; it is a mystery," Abhorson replied.

"Painting, sir, I have heard say, is a mystery," Pompey said, "and whores, sir, being members of my occupation, use painting, thereby proving my occupation a mystery."

The painting an artist does is definitely skilled labor, but the kind of painting referred to by Pompey was the use of cosmetics.

Pompey continued, "What mystery there should be in hanging, if I should be hanged, I cannot imagine."

Abhorson repeated, "Sir, it is a mystery."

"Give me proof," Pompey requested. "Give me a good argument that it is a mystery."

Abhorson attempted to do so:

"An executioner is a thief because he steals a man's life.

"A thief steals clothing — and the executioner keeps the clothing of each person he executes.

"Every true man's apparel fits the thief. If the clothing is too little [in size] for your thief, your true man thinks it big [valuable] enough. If the clothing is too big [in size] for your thief, your thief thinks it little [not as much as he would like to have] enough. Therefore, every true man's apparel fits the thief.

"If the work of the thief is a mystery, then the work of the executioner is a mystery because the thief and the executioner are analogous.

"If the meaning of my words is mysterious to you, that is additional proof that the work of an executioner is a mystery."

The Provost entered the room and asked Pompey, "Are you willing to be an executioner tomorrow?"

Pompey replied, "Sir, I will serve him. I find that being a hangman is a more penitent trade than being a bawd; he asks forgiveness more often."

This was true. Before performing his duty, the executioner always asked the criminal to forgive him.

"You must provide your own chopping block and your own axe to do your duty — behead a criminal — tomorrow at four o'clock," the Provost said to Pompey.

"Come on, bawd," Abhorson said. "I will teach you the mysteries of my trade. Follow me."

"I desire to learn, sir," Pompey replied, "and I hope, if you have occasion to use me for your own turn, you shall find me ready; because truly, sir, for your kindness I owe you a good turn."

One good turn deserves another. In their society, one of the meanings of the phrase "to turn" was "to execute." Pompey was joking that if he ever had to execute the executioner that he would be ready to do it well.

The Provost ordered, "Tell Barnardine and Claudio to come and talk to me."

Pompey and Abhorson departed to carry out the errand.

The Provost said to himself, "Claudio has my pity, but Barnardine, who is a murderer, gets not a jot of pity from me. If the murderer were my own brother, he would get no pity from me."

Claudio entered the room, and the Provost showed him a document and said, "Look, here's the warrant, Claudio, for your death. It is now exactly midnight, and by eight in the morning your body must die and you must become an immortal spirit. Where's Barnardine?"

"He is as fast asleep as a guiltless laborer or a traveler with weary bones. He will not wake up."

"Who can have any good effect on him?" the Provost asked, not expecting a reply. He added, "Well, go; prepare yourself."

Knocking sounded.

The Provost said, "What is that noise?"

He then said to Claudio, "May Heaven give your spirits comfort!"

Claudio exited.

The Provost said, "Coming! I hope it is some pardon or reprieve for the most gentle Claudio."

The Provost did not have to answer the door because Duke Vincentio, still in disguise, opened it and entered the room.

"Welcome, father," the Provost said.

"May the best and most wholesome spirits of the night envelope you, good Provost! Who has come here recently?"

"No one has come here since the bell for curfew rang in the evening."

"Isabella has not been here?"

"No."

"Some people will arrive, then, before too much longer."

"Is there any possibility of a pardon or reprieve for Claudio?"

"There's always hope."

"Angelo is a severe and cruel deputy."

The disguised Duke Vincentio replied, "No, no. Angelo's life is consistent with the written and ruled decrees of his great justice. He subdues with holy abstinence the faults in himself that he spurs on his power to judge in others; were he stained with the same faults that he judges, then he would be a tyrant, but since he is without fault, he is a just ruler."

The disguised Duke Vincentio knew that Angelo, like all men, had sinned. Unlike some men, Angelo was also a hypocrite. However, the disguised Duke Vincentio expected that a pardon for Claudio would come at any minute. He expected Angelo to keep the promise that he had made to Isabella.

Knocking sounded.

"Now some people have come," the disguised Duke Vincentio said. He thought that the pardon had arrived.

The Provost exited, and the disguised Duke Vincentio said to himself, "This is a good and gentle Provost. It is seldom that the hardened jailer is the friend of prisoners and treats them well."

More knocking sounded.

The disguised Duke Vincentio said to himself, "What's going on? That is quite a lot of noise. Whoever is wounding the unassisting and resisting back door with these strokes is possessed with haste and urgency."

The Provost came back and said, "An officer will arrive with the key and let the knocker in. The knocker will have to stay outside until the officer arrives."

"Have you no countermanding order for Claudio yet?" the disguised Duke Vincentio asked the Provost. "Is he still scheduled to die?"

"I have received no countermanding order."

"It is close to dawn," the disguised Duke Vincentio said to the Provost, "but I tell you that you shall hear some news before morning."

"I hope that you know something good," the Provost replied, "yet I believe that no countermanding order will come. We have had no examples of leniency. Besides, on the very seat of judgment Lord Angelo has publicly said that there shall be no leniency for Claudio."

A messenger entered the room; the officer the Provost had summoned had let him in.

The Provost said, "This is Lord Angelo's messenger."

The disguised Duke Vincentio said, "And here comes Claudio's pardon."

The messenger gave the Provost a piece of paper and said, "Lord Angelo has sent you this note; and by me he has sent this further order, that you swerve not from the smallest article of it, neither in time, matter, or other circumstance. Good morning; for, as I take it, it is almost day."

"I shall obey him," the Provost replied.

The messenger exited.

The disguised Duke Vincentio thought, *This is Claudio's pardon, given by a pardoner who is guilty of the same sin as Claudio. Offense is quickly pardoned when high authority is guilty of that offense: When the guilty give pardons, a wide scope of pardons is given. Because the sin is loved, the sinner is befriended.*

He asked out loud, "Now, sir, what is the news?"

"It is exactly as I said earlier: Claudio will be given no pardon," the Provost replied. "In fact, Lord Angelo, who seems to think that I will be remiss in doing my duty, awakens me with this unwonted urging to do my duty. I think that this is strange because he has never done this before."

"Please, read the note to me."

The Provost read the note out loud: "*No matter what you may hear to the contrary, have Claudio executed by four o'clock in the morning; and in the afternoon have Barnardine executed. To assure me that you have done your duty, send Claudio's head to me by five. Let this be duly performed; be aware that more depends on it than we can tell you now. Therefore, do not fail to do your duty. If you fail to do it, you do so at your peril.*"

The Provost asked, "What do you think about this, sir?"

"Who is this Barnardine who is to be executed in the afternoon?" the disguised Duke Vincentio asked.

"He was born in Bohemia, but he was raised here. He has been a prisoner for nine years."

"Nine years! Why didn't the absent Duke either set him free or execute him? I have heard that it was his custom to not long delay in such matters."

"Barnardine's friends constantly got reprieves for him, and until now, in the government of Lord Angelo, it was not definitely proven that he had committed the crime that he was accused of."

"It has now been proven?"

"Most definitely, and he himself does not deny committing the crime."

"Has he been penitent in prison?" the disguised Duke Vincentio asked. "How has he been affected by being in prison?"

"He is a man who fears death no more dreadfully than he fears a drunken sleep; he is without worries, and he is reckless and fearless of what's past, present, or to come. He is oblivious when it comes to life and death, and he is in a state of mortal sin."

"He is in need of spiritual counsel."

The Provost replied, "He will hear none. He has always been free to roam around the prison. If he had the opportunity to escape, he would not take it. He is drunk many times a day, and for many days he is entirely drunk. We have very often awakened him, as if we were going to take him to the place of his execution and showed him what seemed to be a warrant for his execution. This did not affect him at all."

"I will ask more about him soon," the disguised Duke Vincentio said. "I look at your brow, Provost, and I see honesty and resoluteness written there. If I am reading your brow incorrectly, my ancient skill and long experience is misleading me; however, with full confidence that I have read your brow correctly, I will take a risk and if I am wrong, put myself in jeopardy.

"Claudio, whom here you have an order to execute, is no greater forfeit to the law than Angelo is, who has sentenced him. Both of them are guilty of committing the same crime. To make you understand this with a clear demonstration that what I have said is true, I need a respite of only four days. To get me that respite, I want you to do for me both an immediate and a dangerous favor."

"Please, sir, what favor?"

"I want you to delay death; I want you to not kill Claudio."

"How dare I do that?" the Provost said. "The hour for his execution has been set, and I have a clear command, under penalty, to deliver his head to

Angelo. Unless I carry out his order, I may find myself in Claudio's position — Lord Angelo may have *me* executed!"

"By the vow of my order, I will protect you. Let my instructions be your guide. Let this Barnardine be executed this morning, and his head carried to Angelo."

"Angelo has seen both Claudio and Barnardine, and he will know that it is Barnardine's head."

"Oh, death's a great disguiser," the disguised Duke Vincentio said, "and you can improve the disguise. Shave the head, and tie up the beard; and say that it was the desire of the penitent to have his head be so bared before his death. You know that before an execution the shaving of the head is commonly done — the person being executed wants the ax to quickly slice through the neck without being impeded by long hair. If anything should be the result of your action, other than thanks and good fortune, then by the saint whom I profess, I will plead against it with my life."

"Pardon me, good father," the Provost said. "Doing that is against my oath."

"Who did you swear the oath to: the absent Duke, or the deputy?"

"To the Duke, and to his deputies."

"Would you think that you have committed no offence, if Duke Vincentio were to avouch that what you did was just?"

"Yes, but what is the likelihood of that happening?"

"It is not a likelihood; it is a certainty," the disguised Duke Vincentio said. "Yet since I see that you are afraid, that my friar's robes, integrity, and words cannot with ease persuade you to do this, I will go further than I meant to, so that I can pluck all fears out of you."

He showed the Provost a document and said, "Look, sir, here is the handwriting and the seal of Duke Vincentio. You know his handwriting, I am sure; and his seal is not strange to you."

"I know them both."

"The contents of this document concern the return of Duke Vincentio. You shall soon read it at your pleasure, and you will find that within the next two days he will return here.

"Duke Vincentio's return is something that Angelo does not know about because he this very day will receive letters containing extraordinary news. Perhaps he will read that Duke Vincentio is dead; perhaps he will read that

Duke Vincentio has entered some monastery. However, he will not read that Duke Vincentio will return to Vienna in the next two days.

"Look, the morning star alerts the shepherd that it is time to take the sheep out of the fold and to pasture.

"Don't allow yourself to be bewildered by all these things. Soon you will learn more, and you will understand. Call your executioner, and order him to behead Barnardine. I will give him an immediate confession and help prepare him to go to a better place.

"You are still bewildered, but soon all of your doubts will be completely resolved.

"Come, let's go. It is almost clearly dawn."

In another room of the prison, Pompey said to himself, "I know as many people here as I did when I was in our house of the oldest profession. One would think it was Mistress Overdone's own house of prostitution, because here are many of her old customers.

"First, here's young Master Rash; he rashly borrowed money from an unscrupulous lender who wanted more than the 10 percent interest allowed by law. To get around the law, the unscrupulous lender made Master Rash take part of the loan in commodity. Master Rash paid a certain price for the commodity and was supposed to sell the commodity for ready money. Master Rash paid the lender 197 pounds for brown paper and old, stale ginger, and he sold the brown paper and old, stale ginger for around three pounds. Ginger was not much in demand because the old women, who love ginger, were all dead.

"Then there is here one Master Caper, a dancer, at the suit of Master Threepile, the seller of velvet and fine cloth, for some four suits of peach-colored satin, who now impeaches him as a beggar because he cannot pay for the clothing.

"We also have here young Dizzy, the gambler at dice.

"We also have here young Master Deepvow. Quite a few people here deeply vow to pay back their debts if they are released from prison.

"We also have here young Master Copperspur, whose spurs are made of polished copper, which he hopes that a casual observer will mistake for gold.

"We also have here Master Starvelackey, the rapier-and-dagger man. He fights in the modern style, without a shield, and he is either too cheap or too impoverished to feed his servants well.

"We also have here young Dropheir, who killed fat, foolish Pudding. In addition to killing people, Dropheir takes advantage of young heirs, lending them money at usurious rates in anticipation of forthcoming inheritances. Often, the heir drops in wealth because of the loans.

"We also have here Master Forthright the tilter. He enjoys jousting with lances and charges forward on his horse.

"We also have here the brave Master Shoetie, the great traveller who ties his shoes with a yard and a quarter of ribbon in the most extravagant style.

"We also have here wild Halfcan, who drank half a beer, thought himself wildly drunk, and stabbed Pots, the server of beer.

"We also have here, I think, forty more people I know. All are great fornicators in our trade, and now they cry, 'Give me food for the Lord's sake,' out the prison windows to passersby whom they hope will be charitable."

Abhorson the executioner entered the room and said to Pompey, "Bring Barnardine here."

Pompey shouted, "Master Barnardine! You must rise and be hanged. Master Barnardine!"

Abhorson also shouted, "Barnardine!"

Barnardine, who had been asleep, shouted back, "A pox on your throats! Go and catch the plague! Who is making that noise there? Who are you?"

"We are your friends, sir, including the hangman," Pompey replied. "You must be so good, sir, as to rise and be put to death."

Barnardine shouted back, "Go away, you rogue, go away! I am sleepy."

Abhorson said, "Tell him he must wake up, and that quickly, too."

Pompey shouted, "Please, Master Barnardine, wake up and stay awake until you are executed, and sleep afterwards."

Abhorson said, "Go in to him, and fetch him out."

"He is coming, sir, he is coming," Pompey said. "I hear the straw of his bed rustle."

"Is the axe upon the chopping block?" Abhorson asked.

"Everything is very ready, sir."

Barnardine entered the room and said, "How are you now, Abhorson? What's the news with you?"

"Truly, sir," Abhorson replied. "I want you to quickly start your prayers because, you see, the warrant for your execution has come."

"You rogue, I have been drinking all night; I am not ready to die," Barnardine said.

"Actually, you are very ready to die," Pompey said. "Anyone who drinks all night, and is hanged early in the morning, may sleep all the sounder the next day."

"Look, Barnardine, sir; here comes your ghostly — spiritual — father. Do you think now that we are jesting?"

Duke Vincentio, still disguised as a friar, entered the room and said to Barnardine, "Sir, induced by my charity, and hearing how hastily you are to depart from this life, I have come to advise you, comfort you, and pray with you."

"Friar, you do not need to advise, comfort, and pray with me," Barnardine said. "I have been drinking hard all night, and I demand to have more time to prepare myself to die. If they will not give me more time, then they will have to beat out my brains with cudgels. I will not consent to die this day, that's certain. Today I will not be hung or be beheaded."

"But, sir, you must," the disguised Duke Vincentio said, "and therefore I beg you to prepare for the journey you must go."

"I swear I will not die today no matter what any man says."

"Listen to me."

"Not a word," Barnardine replied. "If you have anything to say to me, come to my ward; for from there I will not go today."

Barnardine exited.

The disguised Duke Vincentio said, "Barnardine is not fit either to live or to die. His stony heart is made of gravel! Go after him, fellows; bring him to the block so his head can be chopped off."

Abhorson and Pompey went after Barnardine.

The Provost entered the room and asked, "Now, sir, how do you find the prisoner?"

The disguised Duke Vincentio replied, "Barnardine is a creature unprepared and unfit for death. To transport him in the mind and state he is in now would be damnable because he will certainly be damned."

The Provost said, "Here in the prison, father, there died this morning from a cruel fever a man named Ragozine, who was a most notorious pirate. He is the same age as Claudio; his beard and hair are the same color as Claudio's. What if we ignore this reprobate named Barnardine until he is well inclined and consents to die, and instead give Angelo the head of Ragozine, who resembles Claudio much more than Barnardine does?"

"Oh, this is a welcome accident that Heaven provides!" the disguised Duke Vincentio said. "Send Ragozine's head to Angelo quickly. The hour is quickly coming that Angelo set for Claudio's death. See that this is done and the head sent just as Angelo ordered you to do. Meanwhile, I will persuade this rude wretch to die willingly."

"This shall be done, good father, immediately," the Provost said. "But Barnardine must die this afternoon. How shall we keep Claudio alive *and* save me from the danger that might come if it were known that he is still alive?"

"Let this be done," the disguised Duke Vincentio said. "Put both Barnardine and Claudio in secret cells. Before the Sun has made his daily greeting in the morning twice to the people outside this prison, you shall most definitely find that you are safe from persecution by Angelo."

"I am your willing servant," the Provost said.

"Quick, do what needs to be done, and send the head of Ragozine to Angelo."

The Provost exited.

The disguised Duke Vincentio said to himself, "Now I will write letters to Angelo — the Provost shall carry the letters to him. The letters will tell Angelo that I am close to home, and that, for good reasons, I am bound to enter publicly. I will order Angelo to meet me at the consecrated spring a league from the city; and from there, coolly, step by step, and with due observance of all things necessary, we shall proceed with Angelo."

The Provost returned, carrying the head of Ragozine.

He said, "Here is the head; I'll carry it to Angelo myself."

"This is convenient," the disguised Duke Vincentio said. "Make a swift return because I want to talk with you about such things that no ears but yours should hear."

"I will return as quickly as I can."

He exited.

Isabella came to the door and said, "May Peace be found here!"

The disguised Duke Vincentio said to himself, "That is the voice of Isabella. She's come to know if her brother's pardon has come here yet; however, I will keep her ignorant that her brother is still alive. I will change her despair to Heavenly comforts when she least expects it."

Duke Vincentio had a plan. He wanted Isabella to publicly accuse Angelo. In order for her to do that with the proper passion and fury, she would have to believe that Angelo had murdered her brother. That way, Angelo's crimes would be revealed.

Isabella entered the room and said, "Here I am, with your permission."

"Good morning to you, fair and gracious daughter."

"The greeting is all the better because it was given to me by so holy a man," Isabella replied. "Has Angelo sent my brother's pardon yet?"

"Angelo has released Claudio, Isabella, from the world: An axe took off his head, which has been sent to Angelo."

"No!" Isabella shrieked. "That is not possible!"

"Nothing else has occurred but what I told you," the disguised Duke Vincentio said. "Show that you are wise, daughter, by quietly enduring this."

"Oh, I will go to Angelo and pluck out his eyes!" she said, crying.

"You shall not be admitted to his sight."

"Unhappy Claudio! Wretched Isabella! Injurious world! Most damned Angelo!"

"This neither hurts him nor helps you even a little," the disguised Duke Vincentio said. "Stop crying out therefore; give your cause to Heaven. Listen to what I say, every syllable of which you shall find to be faithful and true.

"Duke Vincentio is coming home to Vienna — Isabella, dry your tears. A member of our convent, who is Duke Vincentio's confessor, told me this news. Already he has carried notice of Duke Vincentio's return to Escalus and Angelo, who are preparing to meet him at the gates of Vienna. There they will give up their power. If you can, put your wisdom on that good path that I would wish it to go. If you do, you shall get what your heart most desires. You will punish Angelo, get the friendship of Duke Vincentio, get as much revenge as you want, and gain general honor."

"I will do as you wish," Isabella replied.

The disguised Duke Vincentio gave her a letter and said, "Give this letter to Friar Peter. It is he who sent me news of Duke Vincentio's return. Say, by this token, that I desire his company at Mariana's house tonight. Her cause and yours I'll give him full information about, and he shall bring you before Duke Vincentio, and you can accuse Angelo of all his crimes while you are face to face with him.

"As for my poor self, I am strongly bound by a sacred vow and shall be absent. Go now with this letter. Take command of your cheek-staining tears and give yourself a light heart. Never trust my holy order, if I have misled you about what will happen."

He heard a noise and asked, "Who's here?"

Lucio entered the room and said, "Good day, all. Friar, where's the Provost?"

"He is not here, sir."

Lucio said, "Oh, pretty Isabella, I am pale at heart to see your eyes so red. You must control yourself.

"I myself am compelled to dine and sup with water and bran; it is my punishment for lechery. I dare not fill my belly because of the punishment that would await me — I would lose my head. One good and fruitful meal would make me horny, and another act of lechery would make me headless. Truly, Isabella, I loved and respected your brother. If the old and eccentric Duke Vincentio — a Duke who knew dark corners — had been in Vienna, your brother would still be alive."

Isabella exited.

The disguised Duke Vincentio said to Lucio, "Sir, the Duke would thank you but little for your reports of his doings in dark corners; the best thing about them is that they are completely incorrect."

"Friar, you don't know Duke Vincentio as well as I do. He's a better woodman — chaser of skirts — than you take him for."

"Well, you'll pay the penalty for what you say about him one day. Fare you well."

"No, wait; I'll go along with you and give you company," Lucio replied. "I can tell you pretty tales about Duke Vincentio."

"You have told me too many stories about him already, sir, if they are true; if they are not true, none would have been enough."

"I once appeared in court before him for getting a wench with child," Lucio said.

"Were you guilty?"

"Yes, I was, but I lied about it under oath. I was forced to lie; otherwise, they would have married me to the rotten medlar."

The word "medlar" was used as a term for prostitutes. A medlar was an apple that was eaten when it was half-rotten.

"Sir, your company is fairer than honest," the disguised Duke Vincentio said. "You dress better than you speak. Rest you well."

"Indeed, I'll go with you to the lane's end," Lucio replied. "If bawdy talk offends you, we'll have very little of it. Friar, I am a kind of burr; I shall stick to you."

Angelo and Escalus talked in a room in Angelo's house.

Escalus said, "Every letter that Duke Vincentio has written has contradicted the letters we have previously received from him."

Claudio replied, "The letters are written in a very uneven and distracted manner. His actions seem to be those of a madman. Let's pray to Heaven that he is not afflicted with a mental disease! And why are we supposed to meet him at the gates and give back to him our commissions and authorities there?"

"I can't imagine."

"And why should we proclaim his return an hour before his entering the city gates, so that if anyone craves redress of injustice, they should exhibit their petitions in the street?"

"He has explained his reasons for that," Escalus said. "He wants to deal with all complaints as soon as he returns. That way, no one will be able to bring them up later."

One reason to deal with complaints earlier instead of later is so that no one could say that Angelo and Escalus had time in which to secretly influence Duke Vincentio to rule in their favor.

"Well, I say to you, let it be proclaimed early in the morning. I'll call upon you at your house. Give notice to such men of high rank and with a retinue of servants as are to meet him."

"I shall, sir. Fare you well," Escalus said.

"Good night," Angelo said.

Escalus exited.

Angelo said to himself, "My evil deed destroys me utterly, and it makes me slow-witted and dull to all proceedings. A deflowered maiden! And deflowered by an eminent person — me — who is charged with enforcing the law against fornication! Except that her tender shame will not allow her to announce publicly that she has lost her virginity, how she could accuse me! Yet reason tells her not to dare to accuse me because my authority as Duke Vincentio's deputy bears such respect and belief that no scandal aimed at me can touch me; instead, the person who charges me with such a scandal will be the one confounded.

"Claudio should have continued to live, except that this riotous youth, with his dangerous passion, might in time to come have taken revenge against me because his dishonored life was ransomed in such a shameful way. But I wish that he were still alive! When we once forget the knowledge of morality that God implanted in us, nothing goes right: We would, and we would not."

Angelo was thinking of Romans 7:19: "For I do not the good thing, which I would, but the evil, which I would not, that do I."

In the fields outside Vienna, Duke Vincentio, who was NOT disguised, and Friar Peter talked.

"At the suitable time, deliver these letters for me," Duke Vincentio said, handing Friar Peter some letters.

Using the royal plural, he continued: "Like you, the Provost knows our purpose and our plot. The plot now being put in action, follow your instructions and always keep in mind the plan that I have formed, although sometimes you may have to swerve from it a little as called for by circumstances.

"Go to Flavius' house, and tell him where I am staying. Give the same information to Valencius, Rowland, and Crassus, and tell them to bring the trumpeters to the gate, but send me Flavius first."

"I shall do it speedily," Friar Peter said.

He departed to carry out his errands.

Varrius, one of Duke Vincentio's friends, walked over to him.

Duke Vincentio said, "I thank you, Varrius; you have made good time. Come, we will walk. Some other of our friends will greet us here soon, my gentle Varrius."

On a street near the city gates, Isabella and Mariana were talking.

"I am loath to speak so inaccurately," Isabella said. "I must allow Angelo to think that he deflowered me. You are the one who must accuse Angelo truthfully. I myself must accuse Angelo incorrectly of deflowering me, Friar Peter said, in order to keep hidden our full plan."

"Do what Friar Peter advises you to do," Mariana said.

"In addition, Friar Peter tells me that if perhaps he should speak against me and seem to be on Angelo's side, that I should not think it strange because it is a medicine that is bitter to swallow but will lead to a sweet end."

"I wish that Friar Peter —" Mariana said.

"Look!" Isabella interrupted. "Here he comes!"

Friar Peter walked over to the two women and said, "Come with me, I have found you a place to stand that is most suitable. You will be in such a position that Duke Vincentio cannot ignore you and pass by you.

"Twice have the trumpets sounded; the highly born and gravest citizens have taken up their positions at the gates, and very soon Duke Vincentio will pass through the gates. Hurry! Let's go!"

CHAPTER 5

— 5.1 —

At the city gate stood Friar Peter, Isabella, and Mariana, who was veiled. Passing through the city gate were Duke Vincentio, Varrius, and some lords. Waiting for Duke Vincentio were Angelo and Escalus. Also present were the Provost, Lucio, many lords, many officers, and many citizens.

Duke Vincentio greeted Angelo, "My very worthy cousin, we are fairly met!"

The two men were not biological cousins; this was simply a courteous way for two noblemen to refer to each other.

Duke Vincentio then greeted Escalus, "Our old and faithful friend, we are glad to see you."

Angelo and Escalus replied together, "May your return bring happiness to your royal grace!"

"I give many and hearty thanks to you both. We have made inquiry about you; and we hear such good things about your justice that I must give you public thanks now, with further reward to follow later."

"You make my obligations to you still greater," Angelo said.

Duke Vincentio replied, "Oh, your desert speaks loudly; and I would wrong it if I were to lock it secretly away in my heart. Your merit deserves to be emblazoned in letters made of brass — a fortified residence against the tooth of time that devours everything and against the erasure that oblivion makes. Your good deeds and justice ought to be remembered. Give me your hand, and let my subjects see me grasping your hand. That way they will know that these outward courtesies would like to proclaim favors that are hidden within my heart."

Duke Vincentio then said, "Come, Escalus, you must walk by us on our other side."

He added, "You two are good supporters."

Friar Peter and Isabella then came forward.

Friar Peter said to Isabella, "Now is the right time: Speak loudly and kneel before Duke Vincentio."

"I ask for justice, royal Duke!" Isabella shouted. "Look down upon a wronged — I would like to have said a virgin! Oh, worthy Prince, do not dishonor your eyes by looking at any other object until you have heard me make my true complaint and you have given me justice, justice, justice, justice!"

Duke Vincentio said, "Tell me your wrongs. In what have you been wronged? By whom have you been wronged? Be brief. Here is Lord Angelo, who shall give you justice. Reveal your complaint to him."

"Oh, worthy Duke Vincentio," Isabella said. "You ask me to seek redemption from the Devil. Hear me yourself because that which I must speak about must either punish me, if I am not believed, or wring redress from you. Hear me! Oh, hear me, here and now!"

"My lord, her wits, I fear, are not firm," Angelo said. "She is mentally unbalanced. She has pleaded to me for her brother's life, which was cut short by course of justice —"

"By course of justice!" Isabella, outraged, shouted.

"— and she will speak most bitterly and strangely against me," Angelo finished.

"Most strangely, but yet most truly, will I speak," Isabella said. "Angelo is guilty of perjury; is it not strange? Angelo is a murderer; is it not strange? Angelo is an adulterous thief, a hypocrite, a virgin-violator; are not these things strange?"

"These things are ten times strange," Duke Vincentio replied.

"It is not truer that he is Angelo than that this is all as true as it is strange. In fact, it is ten times true; for truth is truth to the ultimate degree."

"Take her away!" Duke Vincentio said. "Poor soul, she is saying these things because she is insane."

"Oh, Prince, I beg you, as you believe that there is another comfort than this world — a life after death — please do not neglect and ignore what I say because you believe that I am insane! Do not consider impossible that which only seems to be unlikely. It is not impossible that someone, the wickedest villain on Earth, may seem to be as cautious, as grave, as just, as perfect as Angelo. Likewise, Angelo, in all his robes of office, his insignia, his titles, and his ceremonies, may be an arch-villain. Believe it, royal Prince. If he is less evil than I say he is, he is nothing, but he is more evil than I say he is — I lack more words to describe his evilness."

Duke Vincentio said, "By my honesty, if she is mad — as I believe to be a fact — her madness has the most remarkable coherence of meaning, such a remarkable relationship and connection between one thing and another thing. This is the best logical thinking that I have heard come from an insane person."

"Oh, gracious Duke," Isabella said. "Do not insist that I am insane, and do not banish rational arguments because they do not agree with what most people think about Angelo. Instead, let your reason serve to make the truth appear from where it is hidden, and hide the falsehood that seems to be true."

"Many who are not mad have, surely, a greater lack of reason," Duke Vincentio said. "What do you want to say to me?"

"I am the sister of a man named Claudio," Isabella said. "Because of his act of fornication, he was condemned by Angelo to lose his head. My brother sent me, a novice in a sisterhood, to Angelo. A man named Lucio was my brother's messenger to me —"

Lucio interrupted, "That's me, if it may please your grace. I came to her from Claudio, and I urged her to try her gracious fortune with Lord Angelo to attempt to gain her poor brother's pardon."

"He is the man indeed," Isabella said.

"You were not told to speak," Duke Vincentio said to Lucio.

"No, my good lord," Lucio replied, "nor was I told to stay silent."

"I tell you now to stay silent," Duke Vincentio said. "Please, take note of it, and when you have a matter that concerns you, then pray to Heaven that you know your part well."

"I warrant your honor that I will," Lucio said.

By "warrant," Lucio meant "guarantee."

"If I so order it, the warrant will be for yourself; take heed and be careful," Duke Vincentio said.

By "warrant," Duke Vincentio meant "an order to arrest someone."

Isabella said, "This gentleman told part of my tale —"

Again, Lucio interrupted, "Right."

Duke Vincentio said, "It may be right, but you are in the wrong when you speak before your time."

He said to Isabella, "Proceed."

"I went to this pernicious and contemptible deputy named Angelo —"

"That's somewhat madly spoken," Duke Vincentio said.

"Pardon my language," Isabella said. "The words are appropriate and relevant to the subject matter."

"The apparent madness of speech has been amended again," Duke Vincentio said. "Come to the point. Proceed."

"In brief, setting aside the parts I need not tell, such as how I tried to persuade him, how I prayed to him and kneeled to him, how he denied my request, and how I replied — for all of this took much time — I now begin with grief and shame to tell you the vile conclusion. He would not, except but by gift of my chaste and virgin body to his lascivious and intemperate lust, release my brother; and, after much thought, my sisterly compassion overcame my honor, and I yielded my body to him, but early the next morning, his sexual desire having been satisfied, he sent an order to have my brother beheaded."

"This is very believable!" Duke Vincentio said sarcastically.

"I wish that it were as believable as it is true!" Isabella replied.

"By Heaven, foolish wretch, you do not know what you are saying, or else you have been induced to give false witness in a hateful conspiracy against Angelo's honor," Duke Vincentio said. "First, his integrity stands without blemish. Next, it is not rational that with such vehemence he should punish faults that he has himself committed. If he had so offended, he would have judged your brother the way he judges himself and would not have had him killed. Someone has made you do this. Confess the truth, and say by whose advice you came to lodge a complaint against Angelo."

"And is this all the justice I will get?" Isabella said. "Then, you blessed guardian angels above, help me to be patient, and at the right time reveal the evil that is here hidden behind the perpetrator's position and privilege. May Heaven shield your grace from woe, as I, thus wronged, hence unbelieved go!"

"I know you would like to go," Duke Vincentio said. "An officer! To prison with her! Shall we thus permit an infectious and scandalous breath to fall on Angelo, who is so near and dear to us? This must be a plot. Who knew of your purpose and your coming hither?"

"One whom I wish were here: Friar Lodowick," Isabella replied.

Friar Lodowick was the name that Duke Vincentio used when he was disguised as a friar.

"A ghostly father, probably," Duke Vincentio said. "Who knows this Lodowick?"

The word "ghostly" was ambiguous. It could mean spiritual — or nonexistent.

"My lord, I know him," Lucio replied. "He is a meddling friar; I do not like the man. If he had been a layman, my lord, I would have beaten him soundly because of certain words that he spoke against your grace while you were away from Vienna."

"Words against me?" Duke Vincentio said. "He is a 'good' friar, it seems! And he set on this wretched woman here against Angelo, our deputy! Let this friar be found."

"Only yesterday at night, my lord, I saw her and that friar at the prison. He is a saucy friar, a very impudent and bad fellow."

Friar Peter spoke up and addressed Duke Vincentio: "Blessed be your royal grace! I have stood by, my lord, and I have heard your royal ear abused with lies. First, this woman — Isabella — has very wrongfully accused your deputy, Angelo, who is as free from sexual contact or soil with her as she is free from sexual contact or soil with someone who has not yet been born."

"We believe no less than that," Duke Vincentio said. "Do you know that Friar Lodowick whom she speaks of?"

"I know him to be a man who is divine and holy; he is not scurvy, and he is not a meddler in temporal affairs as this gentleman reported him to be. And, I very definitely know, he is a man who has never said bad things about your grace, as this gentleman reported."

"My lord, Friar Lodowick said the most villainous things about you; believe it," Lucio said.

"Well, Friar Lodowick in time may come to clear himself," Friar Peter said, "but right now he is sick, my lord, of a strange fever. Upon his request, and his request only, because he knew that there would be a complaint made against Lord Angelo, I came here so that I could speak, as if from his mouth, what he knows to be true and what he knows to be false, and what he with his oath and all proofs will make completely clear, whenever he's summoned to appear before you. First, however, let's address the charge made by this woman named Isabella. This worthy nobleman Angelo, whom she so publicly and personally accused, shall be defended. You shall hear what she said disproved in her presence, and she herself shall admit that what she said was untrue."

"Good friar, let's hear the evidence," Duke Vincentio said.

Mariana, still veiled, stepped forward, as guards took Isabella away.

Duke Vincentio said, "Do you not smile at this, Lord Angelo? Oh, Heaven, the vanity of wretched fools!"

He ordered some attendants, "Give us some seats."

He then said, "Cousin Angelo, in this I'll be impartial. I'll let you be the judge in your own case."

He then said, "Is this the witness, Friar Peter? First, let her show her face, and afterward speak."

"Pardon me, my lord," Mariana said. "I will not show my face until my husband asks me to."

"What, are you married?" Duke Vincentio asked.

"No, my lord."

"Are you a virgin?"

"No, my lord."

"A widow, then?"

"Not that, either, my lord."

"Why, you are nothing then: not a virgin, not a widow, and not a wife."

"My lord, she may be a punk," Lucio said, "for many of them are not a maiden, widow, or wife."

"Punk" was a slang word for "prostitute."

"Silence that fellow," Duke Vincentio said. "I wish he had some cause to prattle for himself. He would have cause if he were on trial."

"True, my lord," Lucio said.

"My lord," Mariana said, "I do confess I never was married, and I confess besides that I am no virgin. I have known in the Biblical sense my husband, and yet my husband does not know that he has ever known me."

"He was drunk then, my lord," Lucio said. "It can be nothing else."

"For the benefit of silence, I wish that you were sleeping off a drunk, too!"

"That would keep me quiet, my lord," Lucio said.

"This is no witness for Lord Angelo," Duke Vincentio said. "She has said nothing about him."

"Now I come to the point, my lord," Mariana said. "Isabella, the woman who accuses Angelo of fornication, also in exactly the same way accuses my husband, and charges him, my lord, with committing fornication at such a time that I will swear I had him in my arms as he and I made love."

Angelo asked, "Does Isabella accuse more men than me of committing fornication with her?"

"Not that I know of," Mariana replied.

"No?" Duke Vincentio said. "You say that she accused your husband."

"Why, that is true, my lord, and my husband is Angelo, who thinks he knows that he never knew my body, but who knows he thinks that he knows Isabella's body."

"This is a strange charge," Angelo said. "Let's see your face."

Mariana replied, "My husband tells me to show my face; now I will take off my veil."

She took off her veil and then said, "This is that face, cruel Angelo, that once you swore was worth looking at. This is the hand that, with a vowed contract, was fast locked in yours. This is the body that took away the assignation from Isabella, and this is the body that sexually satisfied you in your garden house. You thought that you were sleeping with Isabella, but you were actually sleeping with me."

"Do you know this woman?" Duke Vincentio asked Angelo.

"Carnally, she says," Lucio said.

"Shut up!" Duke Vincentio ordered.

"I have said enough, my lord," Lucio replied.

"My lord, I must confess that I know this woman," Angelo said. "Five years ago she and I talked about marriage, but the engagement was broken off, in part because the dowry that was promised was not supplied, but mainly because her reputation was ruined because of her lack of chastity — she had light heels, as they said. Since five years ago, I swear upon my faith and honor that I have not spoken to her, seen her, or heard from her."

"Noble Prince," Mariana said, "as there comes light from Heaven and words from breath, as there is sense in truth and truth in virtue, I am affianced this man's wife as strongly as words could make up vows. In addition, my good lord, just last Tuesday night in his garden house he knew me in the Biblical sense as a wife."

The pre-marriage contract between Angelo and Mariana was one that could be broken if the dowry was not paid as agreed, or if the woman was unchaste; however, if the man and woman had sexual relations together, then the two were legally obliged to get married.

Mariana continued: "Since these things are true, let me with safety rise up from my knees or else forever be fixed here — a marble monument!"

Angelo said, "I have until now only smiled contemptuously, but now, my good lord, I ask that you give me the scope and power of justice. My patience here is wounded and irritated. I see that these poor strangely behaving women are no more than the instruments of some mightier member of a conspiracy that sets them on to make these charges against me. Let me have the power, my lord, to uncover this conspiracy."

"Yes, with all my heart," Duke Vincentio said. "Punish them as you please. You foolish friar and you pernicious woman, who are in a plot with Isabella, do you think that your oaths, even if you would swear on each and every saint, would be believable testimonies against Angelo's worth and credit that are ratified by proof?

"You, Lord Escalus, sit with Angelo; lend him your kind help to find out this abusive plot and its source. There is another friar — Friar Lodowick — who made these women make their complaint against Angelo. Let him be sent for."

"I wish that he were here, my lord!" Friar Peter said, "because he indeed had these women make this complaint. Your Provost knows the place where Friar Lodowick lives, and he can fetch him."

"Go do it immediately," Duke Vincentio ordered.

The Provost exited.

Duke Vincentio said, "And you, my noble and well-warranted cousin Angelo, whom it most concerns to hear this matter, do to those who injure you as seems to you best. Give them whatever chastisement you wish. I will leave you for a while. Do not leave until you have well determined how you will treat these slanderers."

Escalus said, "My lord, we'll do our job as judges thoroughly."

Duke Vincentio exited.

Escalus asked, "Signior Lucio, didn't you say that you knew that Friar Lodowick is a dishonest person?"

Lucio replied, "*Cucullus non facit monachum*," which is Latin for "The cowl does not make the monk."

He added, "Friar Lodowick is honest in nothing except in his clothes; he has spoken the most villainous speeches about Duke Vincentio."

"We shall ask you to stay here until he comes so that you can make these charges against him," Escalus said. "This friar seems to be a notoriously bad fellow."

"As any in Vienna, I swear," Lucio said.

"Bring Isabella here again," Escalus said. "I want to speak with her."

An attendant left to get Isabella.

Escalus said to Angelo, "Please, my lord, allow me to question her; you shall see how I'll handle her."

Escalus meant that he would handle her by asking her questions that would reveal the truth, but Lucio pretended to take "handle" in a different — physical — sense.

Lucio said, "You will handle her no better than Angelo, by her own report."

"What did you say?" Escalus asked. "What do you mean?"

"Sir, I think, if you handled her privately, she would sooner confess. Perhaps, if you handle her publicly, she'll be ashamed."

"I will go darkly to work on her," Escalus said.

He meant that the questions would be cunningly designed to trap her and force her to tell the truth. Lucio pretended that "darkly" meant "secretly" and "in the dark."

Lucio said, "That's the way; for women are light at midnight."

The word "light" meant unchaste. Light heels were raised in the air in a position for having sex.

Isabella returned, escorted by officers.

"Come here, Mistress Isabella," Escalus said. "Here is a gentlewoman who denies everything that you have said."

The Provost returned, accompanied by Duke Vincentio, who was once again disguised as a friar: Friar Lodowick.

Lucio said, "My lord, here comes the rascal friar I spoke about, escorted by the Provost."

"He arrives at a very good time," Escalus said. "Do not speak to him until we ask you to."

"I am mum," Lucio replied.

Escalus said to the disguised Duke Vincentio, "Come, sir, did you set these women on to slander Lord Angelo? They have confessed you did."

"It is false."

"What! Do you know where you are?"

"I give respect to your great position in society," the disguised Duke Vincentio said, adding, "Let the Devil sometimes be honored for his burning throne. Normally, we would not honor the Devil, but he has a great position in Hell so sometimes we ought to honor him because of his great position. Where is the Duke? He is the person who should hear me speak."

"The authority of the Duke is invested in us," Escalus said, "and we will hear you speak. Be sure that you speak justly and truly."

"Boldly, at least," the disguised Duke Vincentio said. "But, poor souls, have you come here to ask the fox to give you the sheep? You may say goodbye to your redress — your remedy for a wrong! You will not be able to set things right by acting like this. Is the Duke gone? Then your cause — justice — has been lost, too. The Duke is unjust when he rejects your obviously just appeal — you, Escalus, want justice — and he instead allows the villain whom here you have come to accuse to do the judging in this trial."

Duke Vincentio, while still in disguise, was pointing out that with Angelo acting as judge, justice would not be the result, although Escalus was sincerely attempting to find out the truth and be just. In this particular case, Angelo should be the accused, not the judge.

Lucio said, "This is the rascal; this is the man I spoke of."

"Why, you unreverend and unhallowed friar," Escalus said, "is it not enough that you have suborned these women to falsely accuse this worthy man, Angelo, but with a foul mouth and in his hearing, you call him a villain? And then you turn from him to Duke Vincentio himself and accuse the Duke of injustice?"

He ordered some officers, "Take him away; to the rack with him!"

He looked at the disguised Duke Vincentio and said, "We'll stretch you joint by joint," and then he added so that everyone could hear, "and we will know his purpose."

In a disgusted voice, he said to the disguised Duke Vincentio, "What! You call Duke Vincentio unjust!"

The disguised Duke Vincentio said, "Don't be so angry. The Duke will not dare to stretch this finger of mine any more than he would dare to rack his own finger. I am not his subject, and I am not subject to the local ecclesiastical jurisdiction. My business in this state has made me an observer here in Vienna, where I have seen corruption boil and bubble until it over-ran the stew pots.

You have laws for all faults, but the faults are so ignored and covered up that the strong laws are like the rules posted in a barbershop: They are as much mocked as they are respected."

Barbershops often posted rules on their walls. For example, if someone misbehaved, the punishment might be the pulling of a tooth. The punishments were meant to provoke laughter — no one dealt them out.

"You have slandered the state!" an outraged Escalus said. "Take him to prison!"

"What can you testify against him, Signior Lucio?" Angelo asked. "Is this the man whom you told us about?"

"He is the man, my lord," Lucio said. "Come here, goodman baldpate. Do you know me?"

Lucio called the disguised Duke Vincentio "baldpate" because friars shaved their heads. Duke Vincentio wore a cowl, aka hood, as part of his disguise, and while he was in disguise he kept the hood up to help hide his face.

"I remember you, sir, by the sound of your voice," the disguised Duke Vincentio said.

The hood kept people from seeing the disguised Duke Vincentio's face, but it also interfered with the Duke's seeing other people's faces.

The disguised Duke Vincentio continued, "I met you at the prison, while the Duke was absent."

"Oh, did you?" Lucio said. "And do you remember what you said about the Duke?"

"Very definitely, sir."

"Do you, sir?" Lucio asked. "And do you remember calling the Duke a fleshmonger, a fool, and a coward?"

"You must, sir, change places with me, before you make that my report," the disguised Duke Vincentio said. "You, indeed, called him those things, and others very much worse."

"Oh, you damnable fellow!" Lucio, an inveterate liar, said. "Didn't I grab you by the nose because of what you said?"

"I say that I love the Duke as I love myself," the disguised Duke Vincentio said.

"Listen to what the villain is saying now, after having said his treasonable abuses!" Angelo said.

"We need not talk any longer to him," Escalus said. "Take him to prison! Where is the Provost? Take this friar to prison! Put plenty of fetters on him. Let him speak no more. Take these giglots — these loose women — away, too, and take away the other confederate companion: Friar Peter!"

The disguised Duke Vincentio said to the Provost, "Wait, sir. Wait a while."

Angelo said, "What! Is he resisting arrest? Help arrest him, Lucio."

"Come, sir; come, sir; come, sir," Lucio said. "Damn, sir! Why, you baldpated, lying rascal, you think that you must be hooded, must you? Show us your knave's visage, with a pox on you! Show us your sheep-biting face, and be hanged for an hour! I bet that your hood will come off!"

Lucio pulled down Friar Lodowick's hood, and everyone recognized Duke Vincentio, who said to Lucio, "You are the first knave who ever made a Duke."

Normally, when someone is made a Duke, a member of royalty performs the ceremony, but Lucio, a knave, had made a friar a Duke.

Duke Vincentio said, "First, Provost, let me bail out these gentle three. Isabella, Mariana, and Friar Peter are all innocent."

Lucio attempted to stealthily leave, but Duke Vincentio said to him, "Sneak not away, sir, because Friar Lodowick and you must have a word soon. Lay hold of him and keep him here."

Lucio said, "This may prove worse to me than hanging."

Duke Vincentio said to Escalus, "What you have spoken to me, I pardon. Sit down. I will take Angelo's chair."

He then said to Angelo, "Sir, by your leave."

Angelo stood up, and the Duke sat down.

Duke Vincentio said to Angelo, "Do you have any words, or intelligence, or impudence, that can still do you service? What kind of defense can you make of your actions? If you can make a defense, rely upon it until I tell my story, and then realize that you can make no defense. At that time, confess."

"Oh, my dread lord," Angelo said. "I would be guiltier than my guiltiness if I were to think I can hide my crimes when I perceive that your grace, like power divine, has looked upon them. Therefore, good Prince, no longer let a trial be held and expose my shame. Instead, let my trial be my own confession. All I beg from your grace now is immediate sentencing and death."

Duke Vincentio said, "Come here, Mariana."

He asked Angelo, "Tell me, were you ever contracted to marry this woman?"

"I was, my lord."

"Go and take her away from here, and marry her immediately," Duke Vincentio said. "Friar Peter, you perform the marriage. Once these two are married, bring Angelo back here again. Go with him, Provost."

Angelo, Mariana, Friar Peter, and the Provost exited.

Escalus said, "My lord, I am more amazed at Angelo's dishonor than at the strangeness of it. I did not think that he was capable of such sin."

"Come here, Isabella," Duke Vincentio said. "Your friar is now your Prince. As a friar, I was attentive and devoted to you, and I did my best to help you. I have changed from friar to Duke, but I have not changed my heart. I am still attentive and devoted to you, and I will do my best to help you."

"Give me pardon," Isabella said. "I, your vassal, have caused you pain and trouble."

"You are pardoned, Isabella," Duke Vincentio said. "And now, dear maiden, please be as generous to us. Your brother's death, I know, sits at your heart, and you may wonder why I kept my identity and power hidden as I worked to save his life, instead of simply revealing my identity and power. Because I kept them hidden, your brother was lost."

Of course, Duke Vincentio was lying. Soon he would reveal that Claudio, Isabella's brother, was still alive. By concealing that fact now, he would make Isabella's future happiness greater when she learned that her brother was still alive. In addition, and more importantly, he wanted Angelo to know the enormity of his sin.

Duke Vincentio continued: "Oh, most kind maiden, his death occurred too quickly. I did not think that he would be executed with such swift celerity. It knocked my plan in the head and ruined it. But may peace be with him! A life is a better life when it need not fear death. A life that lives but fears death is not as good. Your brother is enjoying Heaven and will never again die. Let this be your comfort: Your brother is happy in Heaven."

"I am comforted by that, my lord," Isabella replied.

Angelo, Mariana, Friar Peter, and the Provost returned. Angelo and Mariana were now married.

Duke Vincentio said to Isabella, "For Mariana's sake, you must pardon this newly married man who is approaching here, whose lecherous imagination wronged your well-defended honor. He violated you in his imagination although not in reality. But he condemned your brother to death. This made him guilty of two things: violation of sacred chastity, and violation and breach of his promise to set your brother free. By breaching his promise to set your brother free, he became guilty of taking the life of your brother. Because of that crime, the very mercy of the law cries out very audibly, even from Angelo's own tongue, 'An Angelo for a Claudio, a death for a death! Haste always repays haste, and leisure answers leisure. Like requites like, and MEASURE always FOR MEASURE.'"

Duke Vincentio was remembering Exodus 21:23-25: "But if death follow, then thou shalt pay life for life. Eye for eye, tooth for tooth, hand for hand, foot for foot, burning for burning, wound for wound, stripe for stripe."

He was correct when he said that "the very mercy of the law cries out very audibly, even from Angelo's own tongue, 'An Angelo for a Claudio, a death for a death!'"

Earlier, Angelo had said this to Isabella: "I show pity most of all when I show justice because when I show justice I pity those whom I do not know, people whom an unpunished offence would afterwards gall and harm. A criminal who is not punished will commit the same crime again. I also show pity and do right to an offender who, because he is punished for committing one foul wrong, does not live to commit another foul wrong. Be satisfied and restrain yourself. Your brother dies tomorrow. Reconcile yourself to his death."

Duke Vincentio continued: "Angelo, your guilt is evident, and even if you were to ask for mercy, your guilt would still require that you die. We condemn you to go to the very block where Claudio stooped to be beheaded, and with similar haste."

He ordered, "Take Angelo away to be beheaded!"

Mariana said, "Oh, my most gracious lord, I hope you will not mock me by giving me a husband and immediately taking him away from me."

"It is your husband who mocked you with a husband," Duke Vincentio said. "I want to safeguard your honor, and so I thought it fit that you marry Angelo. Otherwise, the news that he has had sex with you might give you a bad reputation and hurt your future life.

"As for his possessions, although they are forfeited to the state because Angelo is a felon, we give them to you along with all widow's rights. Buy yourself a better husband."

"My dear lord," Mariana replied. "I crave no other man, and I crave no better man, than Angelo."

"Do not crave him," Duke Vincentio said. "We have made up our mind that he shall die."

"My gentle liege —" Mariana began, kneeling.

Duke Vincentio interrupted, "You are wasting your words."

He ordered again, "Take Angelo away so that he may die!"

He then said to Lucio, "Now, sir, I turn my attention to you."

"My good lord!" Mariana said.

She then said, "Sweet Isabella, take my part. Lend me your knees, and all my life to come I'll lend you all my life to do you service."

"You are asking Isabella to do something that goes against all sense and reason," Duke Vincentio said. "If she were to kneel down and beg mercy for Angelo, her brother's ghost would break out of the stone of his tomb and take her away in horror of her actions."

"Isabella, sweet Isabella," Mariana begged, "please kneel by me. Hold up your hands, say nothing. I'll speak all that needs to be said. People say that the best men are molded out of faults; their sins keep them from being proud of their virtues. For this reason, and for the most part, they become much better as a result of being a little bad. My husband may also become better as a result of his faults. Oh, Isabella, will you not lend a knee?"

Duke Vincentio said to Isabella, "Angelo dies because he caused Claudio's death."

Isabella remembered the words of Jesus in Matthew 5:38-39: "Ye have heard that it hath been said, An eye for an eye, and a tooth for a tooth. But I say unto you, Resist not evil: but whosoever shall smite thee on thy right cheek, turn to him the other also." New Testament justice is often tempered by mercy.

She said, "Most bounteous sir," and then she knelt.

She continued: "If it please you, look on Angelo, who is condemned by you to die, as if my brother had lived. I in part think that a due sincerity governed Angelo's deeds, until he looked at me and was tempted to sin. Since that is the case, let Angelo not die. My brother received only justice, in that he did the thing for which he died. My brother committed fornication, and he was sentenced to die because he was guilty of fornication.

"As for Angelo, his act did not overtake his bad intent. He wanted to commit fornication with me, but he did not. Because of that, his fault must be buried as being only an intention that perished by the way and did not become reality. Thoughts are not subjects of yours; intentions are merely thoughts. They are not real, existing deeds."

"She is right, my lord," Mariana said.

"Your suit's unprofitable," Duke Vincentio said. "Angelo shall die. Stand up, I say."

He added, "I have thought of another fault. Provost, how did it come to be that Claudio was beheaded at such an unusual hour?"

"It was so commanded," the Provost replied.

"Did you receive a special legal warrant for the deed?"

"No, my good lord; I received a private message," the Provost replied.

"For which I do discharge you of your office," Duke Vincentio said. "Give up your keys."

"Pardon me, noble lord," the Provost said. "I thought it was a fault, but I did not know for sure. I repented the death of Claudio, after more thought. Evidence for what I say can be found in the prison, where a prisoner, whom I was ordered to execute by a private message, is still alive."

"Who is he?" Duke Vincentio asked.

"His name is Barnardine."

"I wish that you had done the same for Claudio what you did for Barnardine. Go and fetch him and bring him here; let me see him."

The Provost exited.

Escalus said, "I am sorry that one as learned and as wise as you have always appeared to be, Lord Angelo, should slip so grossly, both in the heat of passion and in a lack of tempered judgment afterward."

"I am sorry that I have caused such sorrow," Angelo replied, "So deeply does my sorrow stick in my penitent heart that I crave death more than I crave mercy. I deserve death, and I beg for death."

The Provost returned, bringing with him Barnardine, Claudio, and Juliet. Claudio's face was muffled and hidden by his clothing.

"Which one is Barnardine?" Duke Vincentio asked.

The Provost replied, "This is he, my lord," while indicating Barnardine.

"A friar told me about this man," Duke Vincentio said.

Addressing Barnardine, he added, "You are said to have a stubborn soul that sees no further than this world, and you act accordingly. You have been condemned to die; however, I pardon all your Earthly crimes, and I pray that you will respond to this mercy by taking action to gain better times to come, both in this life and in the next.

"Friar Peter, give him spiritual counsel. I leave him in your hands."

Duke Vincentio then asked, "Who is that muffled fellow?"

"This is another prisoner whom I saved," the Provost replied. "He should have died when Claudio lost his head; he greatly resembles Claudio."

The Provost unmuffled Claudio, revealing his face.

Isabella and Mariana stood up, Isabella ran over to Claudio, and they rejoiced.

Duke Vincentio, who knew that this was really Claudio, said, "If he resembles your brother, I pardon him for your brother's sake, and, as for your own lovely sake, give me your hand and say that you will marry me and be mine. He is my brother, too — but there will be a fitter time for us to talk about this marriage proposal.

"Because of this strange appearance of the living Claudio, Lord Angelo perceives he's safe; he knows that he will not be beheaded. I think I see a quickening in his eye.

"Well, Angelo, your evil requites you well: You have a wife. Look that you love your wife; her worth is fully worth yours.

"I find in myself an inclination to pardon people, and yet here's one person whom I cannot pardon."

He said to Lucio, "You have said that you knew me to be a fool, a coward, a lecher, an ass, a madman. What have I done to you that makes you call me such names?"

"Truly, my lord," Lucio said. "It was all a joke. That's just how I talk. I said those things on the spur of the moment, without thinking. I know that you can have me hanged for saying such things, but I prefer a lesser punishment, if it pleases you: Have me whipped, not hanged."

"You shall be whipped first, sir, and hanged afterward," Duke Vincentio said.

He added, "Provost, proclaim around about the city that if any woman has been wronged by this lewd fellow — I myself have heard him swear that he got a woman pregnant — let her appear, and he shall marry her. Once the two have been married, then he shall be whipped and hanged."

"I beg your Highness," Lucio said, "do not marry me to a whore. Your Highness said even now that I made you a Duke. My good lord, do not repay me by making me a cuckold."

"Upon my honor, you shall marry her," Duke Vincentio replied. "However, I pardon your slanders, and therefore you shall not be whipped and hanged — but you shall be married. Take him to prison, and make sure that he is married."

"Marrying a punk — a prostitute — my lord, is very much like being pressed to death, whipping, and hanging," Lucio said.

When a man is pressed to death, he lies on his back on a sharp rock, and heavy weights are placed on a board on his chest. More and more weights are added until the man dies.

"Anyone who slanders a Prince deserves such punishment," Duke Vincentio said.

Some officers took Lucio away to prison.

Duke Vincentio spoke to many people in turn:

"Claudio, make sure that you marry and restore the honor of Juliet, whom you wronged.

"May you have joy, Mariana!

"Love Mariana, Angelo. I have been her confessor, and I know that she is virtuous.

"Thank you, good friend Escalus, for your great goodness. There's more to come. You shall be rewarded with more than mere words.

"Thank you, Provost, for your care and secrecy: You have played your role well. We shall employ you in a worthier place: You shall be promoted.

"Forgive the Provost, Angelo, who brought you the head of Ragozine instead of Claudio's, but this is an offence that pardons itself.

"Dear Isabella, I have a proposal that much concerns your future happiness. If you say yes to my proposal of marriage, what's mine is yours and what's yours is mine."

Using the royal plural, Duke Vincentio then said to everyone, "So, let us all go to our palace; there we'll tell you some things to come that it is fitting that you know."

APPENDIX A: ABOUT THE AUTHOR

It was a dark and stormy night. Suddenly a cry rang out, and on a hot summer night in 1954, Josephine, wife of Carl Bruce, gave birth to a boy — me. Unfortunately, this young married couple allowed Reuben Saturday, Josephine's brother, to name their first-born. Reuben, aka "The Joker," decided that Bruce was a nice name, so he decided to name me Bruce Bruce. I have gone by my middle name — David — ever since.

Being named Bruce David Bruce hasn't been all bad. Bank tellers remember me very quickly, so I don't often have to show an ID. It can be fun in charades, also. When I was a counselor as a teenager at Camp Echoing Hills in Warsaw, Ohio, a fellow counselor gave the signs for "sounds like" and "two words," then she pointed to a bruise on her leg twice. Bruise Bruise? Oh yeah, Bruce Bruce is the answer!

Uncle Reuben, by the way, gave me a haircut when I was in kindergarten. He cut my hair short and shaved a small bald spot on the back of my head. My mother wouldn't let me go to school until the bald spot grew out again.

Of all my brothers and sisters (six in all), I am the only transplant to Athens, Ohio. I was born in Newark, Ohio, and have lived all around Southeastern Ohio. However, I moved to Athens to go to Ohio University and have never left.

At Ohio U, I never could make up my mind whether to major in English or Philosophy, so I got a bachelor's degree with a double major in both areas, then I added a master's degree in English and a master's degree in Philosophy.

Currently, and for a long time to come (I eat fruits and veggies), I am spending my retirement writing books such as *Nadia Comaneci: Perfect 10*, *The Funniest People in Dance*, *Homer's* Iliad: *A Retelling in Prose*, and *William Shakespeare's* Othello: *A Retelling in Prose*.

By the way, my sister Brenda Kennedy writes romances such as *A New Beginning* and *Shattered Dreams*.

APPENDIX B: SOME BOOKS BY DAVID BRUCE

Retellings of a Classic Work of Literature

Arden of Faversham: *A Retelling*

Ben Jonson's The Alchemist: *A Retelling*

Ben Jonson's The Arraignment, or Poetaster: *A Retelling*

Ben Jonson's Bartholomew Fair: *A Retelling*

Ben Jonson's The Case is Altered: *A Retelling*

Ben Jonson's Catiline's Conspiracy: *A Retelling*

Ben Jonson's The Devil is an Ass: *A Retelling*

Ben Jonson's Epicene: *A Retelling*

Ben Jonson's Every Man in His Humor: *A Retelling*

Ben Jonson's Every Man Out of His Humor: *A Retelling*

Ben Jonson's The Fountain of Self-Love, or Cynthia's Revels: *A Retelling*

Ben Jonson's The Magnetic Lady, or Humors Reconciled: *A Retelling*

Ben Jonson's The New Inn, or The Light Heart: *A Retelling*

Ben Jonson's Sejanus' Fall: *A Retelling*

Ben Jonson's The Staple of News: *A Retelling*

Ben Jonson's A Tale of a Tub: *A Retelling*

Ben Jonson's Volpone, or the Fox: *A Retelling*

Christopher Marlowe's Complete Plays: Retellings

Christopher Marlowe's Dido, Queen of Carthage: *A Retelling*

Christopher Marlowe's Doctor Faustus: *Retellings of the 1604 A-Text and of the 1616 B-Text*

Christopher Marlowe's Edward II: *A Retelling*

Christopher Marlowe's The Massacre at Paris: *A Retelling*

Christopher Marlowe's The Rich Jew of Malta: *A Retelling*

Christopher Marlowe's Tamburlaine, Parts 1 and 2: *Retellings*

Dante's Divine Comedy: *A Retelling in Prose*

Dante's Inferno: *A Retelling in Prose*

Dante's Purgatory: *A Retelling in Prose*

Dante's Paradise: *A Retelling in Prose*

The Famous Victories of Henry V: *A Retelling*

From the Iliad *to the* Odyssey: *A Retelling in Prose of Quintus of Smyrna's* Posthomerica

George Chapman, Ben Jonson, and John Marston's Eastward Ho! *A Retelling*

George Peele's The Arraignment of Paris: *A Retelling*

George Peele's The Battle of Alcazar: *A Retelling*

George's Peele's David and Bathsheba, and the Tragedy of Absalom: *A Retelling*

George Peele's Edward I: *A Retelling*

George Peele's The Old Wives' Tale: *A Retelling*

George-a-Greene: *A Retelling*

The History of King Leir: *A Retelling*

Homer's Iliad: *A Retelling in Prose*

Homer's Odyssey: *A Retelling in Prose*

J.W. Gent.'s The Valiant Scot: *A Retelling*

Jason and the Argonauts: A Retelling in Prose of Apollonius of Rhodes' Argonautica

John Ford: Eight Plays Translated into Modern English

John Ford's The Broken Heart: *A Retelling*

John Ford's The Fancies, Chaste and Noble: *A Retelling*

John Ford's The Lady's Trial: *A Retelling*

John Ford's The Lover's Melancholy: *A Retelling*

John Ford's Love's Sacrifice: *A Retelling*

John Ford's Perkin Warbeck: *A Retelling*

John Ford's The Queen: *A Retelling*

John Ford's 'Tis Pity She's a Whore: *A Retelling*

John Lyly's Campaspe: *A Retelling*

John Lyly's Endymion, The Man in the Moon: *A Retelling*

John Lyly's Galatea: *A Retelling*

John Lyly's Love's Metamorphosis: *A Retelling*

John Lyly's Midas: *A Retelling*

John Lyly's Mother Bombie: *A Retelling*

John Lyly's Sappho and Phao: *A Retelling*

John Lyly's The Woman in the Moon: *A Retelling*

John Webster's The White Devil: *A Retelling*

King Edward III: *A Retelling*

Mankind: *A Medieval Morality Play* (A Retelling)

Margaret Cavendish's The Unnatural Tragedy: *A Retelling*

The Merry Devil of Edmonton: *A Retelling*

The Summoning of Everyman: *A Medieval Morality Play* (A Retelling)

Robert Greene's Friar Bacon and Friar Bungay: *A Retelling*

The Taming of a Shrew: *A Retelling*

Tarlton's Jests: A Retelling

Thomas Middleton's A Chaste Maid in Cheapside: *A Retelling*

Thomas Middleton's Women Beware Women: *A Retelling*

Thomas Middleton and Thomas Dekker's The Roaring Girl: *A Retelling*

Thomas Middleton and William Rowley's The Changeling: *A Retelling*

The Trojan War and Its Aftermath: Four Ancient Epic Poems

Virgil's Aeneid: *A Retelling in Prose*

William Shakespeare's 5 Late Romances: Retellings in Prose

William Shakespeare's 10 Histories: Retellings in Prose

William Shakespeare's 11 Tragedies: Retellings in Prose

William Shakespeare's 12 Comedies: Retellings in Prose

William Shakespeare's 38 Plays: Retellings in Prose
William Shakespeare's 1 Henry IV, aka Henry IV, Part 1: *A Retelling in Prose*
William Shakespeare's 2 Henry IV, aka Henry IV, Part 2: *A Retelling in Prose*
William Shakespeare's 1 Henry VI, aka Henry VI, Part 1: *A Retelling in Prose*
William Shakespeare's 2 Henry VI, aka Henry VI, Part 2: *A Retelling in Prose*
William Shakespeare's 3 Henry VI, aka Henry VI, Part 3: *A Retelling in Prose*
William Shakespeare's All's Well that Ends Well: *A Retelling in Prose*
William Shakespeare's Antony and Cleopatra: *A Retelling in Prose*
William Shakespeare's As You Like It: *A Retelling in Prose*
William Shakespeare's The Comedy of Errors: *A Retelling in Prose*
William Shakespeare's Coriolanus: *A Retelling in Prose*
William Shakespeare's Cymbeline: *A Retelling in Prose*
William Shakespeare's Hamlet: *A Retelling in Prose*
William Shakespeare's Henry V: *A Retelling in Prose*
William Shakespeare's Henry VIII: *A Retelling in Prose*
William Shakespeare's Julius Caesar: *A Retelling in Prose*
William Shakespeare's King John: *A Retelling in Prose*
William Shakespeare's King Lear: *A Retelling in Prose*
William Shakespeare's Love's Labor's Lost: *A Retelling in Prose*
William Shakespeare's Macbeth: *A Retelling in Prose*
William Shakespeare's Measure for Measure: *A Retelling in Prose*
William Shakespeare's The Merchant of Venice: *A Retelling in Prose*
William Shakespeare's The Merry Wives of Windsor: *A Retelling in Prose*
William Shakespeare's A Midsummer Night's Dream: *A Retelling in Prose*
William Shakespeare's Much Ado About Nothing: *A Retelling in Prose*
William Shakespeare's Othello: *A Retelling in Prose*
William Shakespeare's Pericles, Prince of Tyre: *A Retelling in Prose*
William Shakespeare's Richard II: *A Retelling in Prose*
William Shakespeare's Richard III: *A Retelling in Prose*
William Shakespeare's Romeo and Juliet: *A Retelling in Prose*
William Shakespeare's The Taming of the Shrew: *A Retelling in Prose*
William Shakespeare's The Tempest: *A Retelling in Prose*
William Shakespeare's Timon of Athens: *A Retelling in Prose*
William Shakespeare's Titus Andronicus: *A Retelling in Prose*
William Shakespeare's Troilus and Cressida: *A Retelling in Prose*
William Shakespeare's Twelfth Night: *A Retelling in Prose*
William Shakespeare's The Two Gentlemen of Verona: *A Retelling in Prose*
William Shakespeare's The Two Noble Kinsmen: *A Retelling in Prose*
William Shakespeare's The Winter's Tale: *A Retelling in Prose*